JUDGMENT DAY

& OTHER WHITE LIES

To Matt:

"Like we can't ever get a
guilty verdict when a pig admits
to being a pig on Live TV." Hope
you enjoy the book! Been
nice getting to know you
online.
With
love,

JUDGMENT DAY

& OTHER WHITE LIES

by ~~Mike Hilbig~~

MADVILLE
P U B L I S H I N G

LAKE DALLAS, TEXAS

FIRST EDITION

Judgment Day & Other White Lies is a work of fiction. Names, characters, places, and incidents either are the products of the author's imagination or are used fictitiously. Any resemblance to actual events, locales, businesses, companies, or persons, living or dead, is entirely coincidental.

ACKNOWLEDGMENTS:
"The Bell Witch Hunter & the Curse of Jasksonian History" in
The Packingtown Review, Vol. 12, Fall 2019.

Requests for permission to reprint material from this work
should be sent to:

Permissions
Madville Publishing
P.O. Box 358
Lake Dallas, TX 75065

Author Photograph: Leslie Cook
Cover Art: Crowcrumbs, Crowcrumbs.com

ISBN: 978-1-948692-76-2 paperback, 978-1-948692-77-9 ebook
Library of Congress Control Number: 2021941083

Contents

For Leslie

The Para(Fa)ble of the Stoned Ape

"Before the beginning of everything, and by everything, I mean before humans were around to invent the beginning, so like before that, there were these apes who got pushed out of the jungle, found themselves roaming across the plains and prairies tracking and hunting this prehistoric form of cattle who were always shitting all over the place, leaving behind massive prehistoric-sized cow patties, which were fertile ground for magic mushrooms to sprout. Anyway, these monkeys, aside from cattle, they liked to eat bugs—big slimy salty bugs—bugs who fed on the same cow shit—considered the best delicacy in what they did not yet consider a world. So while these monkeys were out hunting, they'd dig around in the cow shit harvesting bugs, unknowingly eating mushroom spores, about what we might think of as a micro-dose nowadays, anyway, point is, the new diet gave them better focus and vision. All of a sudden they're tracking these cattle better than they ever have, they're eating more red meat, they're eating more shitbugs, and also more magic mushroom spores. Eventually, this new focus helps them figure out that the mushroom spores are responsible for their progress, so to speak, and not the shitbugs. Then they figure out that the spores grow into mushrooms, which have a more potent effect, so now they're looking for mushrooms first and shitbugs second, which means they're hunting way better than before,

1

they're eating even more red meat, and the combination of extra psilocybin and complex proteins has them all kinds of aroused. Basically, these monkeys, they just start fucking like crazy, all over the prairie. It's hunt by day, orgy by night, all just humping each other, male, female, doesn't matter which is which, one ape to another, to another, to another, finding all sorts of ways that bodies fit together, rubbing, licking, sucking, probing, no partners, they were having a singular experience, rampant group sex or pack masturbation, however you want to figure.

"So they start having more offspring with more genetic variation, and this singular pack grows larger and creates even better hunters who can find even more mushrooms. Soon after, they're eating what would seem like excessive amounts of mushrooms, and they're noticing the stars in the sky for the first time—since before the mushrooms the sky felt more like something worth ignoring in the background, like wallpaper or whatever—anyway, one day, they're on this trip and there's this big other thing out there in that starry sky, this thing breathing at them, and they realize they've been this little pack of apes on this little piece of land hunting and fucking without any awareness of the vast space and time they now know they're a part of. So one looks at another with this huge grin, because he can't think of why he hasn't thought of it before, and he wants to tell her about everything and nothing all at the same time, about self and other, about life and death, about man and woman, but all he can say is, 'Holy shit, I'm so fucked up,' to which she replies, 'Yeah, me too,' because she can understand what he means even though he hasn't said it yet, and they laugh a great laugh and hear difference there, and all of this was actually way more revelatory than it seems because it was the first time anyone had a conversation. So now they're communicating, and they're not apes anymore but some form of early apepeople, and they develop more language and they keep eating those mushrooms and they start telling stories about their trips, and they start calling that big other thing God, and they become some other civilization that sees how alone they are in what they now call the world, separated from that singular pack by form and distance. So now these apepeople start organizing into the societies that will become humanity, telling each other similar stories that are also different, and some of them write those stories down for those who come after, and some who come after model their stories off of those that were written down before, anyway, point is, now we're all living by these mythologies that are really nothing more than increasingly complex versions of those first descriptions of the hallucinations of a bunch of violent, sex-crazed, stoned monkeys."

"Some story you got there."

"That's all you have to say?"

"What else should I say?"

"I mean, I'd say it makes a lot of sense."

"Hmmm."

"A lot of our ideas still seem to come from violent, sex-crazed, stoned monkeys. I mean, look at who we elected president. Anyway, I'm not sure the story's right or anything, but I will say the theory behind it seems to support the reality that we're programmed to gain more instantaneous and intense pleasure from fucking and getting high than we do from anything else, and maybe it's because, at the core of everything, in more ways than just the obvious, it's where we really do come from."

"Seems kind of full of shit to me."

"I didn't make it up. McKenna did."

"Who?"

"Terrance McKenna. You know, the druggie pseudo-scientist in that documentary we watched?"

"Yeah, that guy. He's as full of shit as those apes of his."

"We all are. That's his whole point. That full-of-shitness has a directly proportional relationship to the desire to tell stories. That we're all just making it all up as we go along, hoping we'll be better people if we just get into a better diet, or a better set of habits, or some kinky sex thing, or whatever. That when it really boils down to it, evolution is just a spore creating the fungus of progress, feeding itself on a steaming pile of excess, ever-becoming history's paradoxically both finished and unfinished product."

Fury, or a Matricide in Sound

Orestes heard his mother straining to moan behind him in the living room. As he crossed over the threshold from the scratched-up hardwood—through the beaded curtain—and onto the black-and-used-to-be-white checkerboard tiles in the kitchen, he turned his head over his shoulder and yelled out, "It'll be ready in a few."

Then silence.

"Dawn? Are you okay?"

The words of her reply were lost in the cacophony of an echo of pain, but judging from the higher pitch of the sound she finally made, he assumed she affirmed his actions. He reached into the cabinet above the sink, again registering but not really hearing the slow leak—*plop, plop, plop*—the rhythm a subliminal reminder of time's inevitable passing—*plop, plop, plop*. He pulled out a translucent orange bottle, opened it, dumped every last pill into the mortar sitting on the counter's fading maroon tiles. Ground up the morphine with a pestle. He'd been given the apothecary set as a gift the last time his band The Libation Bearers had been out on tour, at a stop in Monterrey, a roadside vendor saw him eyeing it. He was a huge fan of Orestes' guitar work and gave the gift free of charge. Orestes returned the favor by letting the man come backstage after the show the next night. He had intended to use the *molcajete*, as the vendor had called it, for crushing garlic, onions and herbs, but it had remained all these years on the shelf collecting dust, just like the rest of his life. Now, giving the stoneware its first test run, staring into a mound of baby blue powder freshly dusting the concave surface, he felt a connection to the spirits of his ancestors. He knew there was some kind of mysterious force, he didn't want to call it God, but some ineffable thing, some great inner voice, had called him to play the ancient role of medicine man—*plop, plop, plop.*

He reached back up into the cabinet, brought down a bottle of Bulleit and a plastic sippie cup with a lid. He opened the drawer and took out a sterling silver spoon, which was stained bronze from one or two—or who knows how many—washes with hard city water and strong detergent. He unscrewed the lid from the cup, scooped up the morphine and dumped it inside before pouring three fingers of bourbon on top. Then he threw in a handful of rocks from the freezer, topped it off with water, and stirred as if only artificial sweetener into a glass of tea. He tapped the spoon—*clack, clack*—against the threaded rim, the resulting concoction a NyQuil green, the admixture complete—*plop, plop, plop.* He screwed back on the lid. Oughta do the trick, he thought.

He walked back out of the kitchen—through the dining nook—past the card table barely holding up under the weight of a mountain of medical bills—and back into the living room where all this began (at least this time around) and would now end. Saw his mother sitting in bed, the back tilted up. They'd purchased the hospital bed from a private seller off of Craig's List. It was a steal, cheap because the previous owner had died in it. Only way he could afford a bed like that with his meagerly pay from Autozone and the spare change he brought home from playing gigs. They were lucky to get anything at all, no money to put Dawn into any kind of a medical facility, the funding never came through, her Medicaid application rejected, not even the government would cover pre-existing conditions these days, despite all the Congresspeople claiming they did so in varying convoluted types of ways. The bed was supposed to provide the slightest semblance of sanitation, the illusion of well-being, but as he looked around at the concert posters tacked up with corners missing, the dust caked up on the ancient ceiling fan he couldn't even turn on for fear of it falling, the rusted out space heater in the wall—one of numerous violations of city code, a bomb in the making— he knew it was never the right environment for this sort of thing, had never been a good idea. Here she sat, her legs, feet, wrists, and partially amputated hands wrapped in bandages covering but not hiding the ever-present rotted and infected wounds. He'd never wrap them for her again. A blessing and a curse. This woman who'd raised him and then abandoned him and would soon abandon him again, for good (sort of— was more complicated than that—as it always is).

Orestes pulled out a built-in tray-table from the side panel of the bed and suspended it over the top of Dawn's ever-shrinking waistline. Set the cocktail on top. He walked over to his turntable, at the knee-high entertainment center, which was really a plank suspended across two concrete blocks, placed above an amp and a mixer, sitting in-between the two plexiglass speaker boxes, each containing two twelve-inch speakers and both littered with creams, rubs, and scented candles across the tops of their carpeted surfaces. He bent down and pulled a record out of its sleeve from a milk crate next to the mixer. He chose The Beatles' *Revolver*, a shared favorite, and applied a dab of vinyl cleaner before lightly sweeping the brush from the center outward and then blowing on the record. He fanned it through the air before placing it B-side up on the turntable and hitting the button for the automatic arm. He watched it pick up, swing to the left and drop its diamond needle down onto the outer groove. Good Day Sunshine. She started laughing, then coughing, a few tears fell. She hadn't touched her drink yet. He asked what seemed like a simultaneously dumb and obligatory question, "Sure you're ready?"

She picked up the cup with the three remaining fingers on her right hand and shakily maneuvered it to her lips. Took a long sip before giving both a trite and meaningful answer, "More than you could ever know."

The response stung worse than it should have. He sat on the edge of the bed and probed her with a longing stare. Wanted some sort of apology—not that she hadn't apologized before, but it never felt *final* for some reason. Could never tell how much she *meant* it. He wanted to know.

Then again, his response to her response, the way his chiseled jaw bone seemed to crack and ripple before her eyes, his display of disapproval, had stung her just as bad. She kept her eyes level with his gaze, not breaking, she might have lost his respect, but she wouldn't lose a staring contest, not right now, not with her son. The way she saw it, life was just a never-ending series of shifting and intersecting points-of-view, written into somebody else's story. Surely no different for the two of them. She knew what she was and wasn't guilty of on some days, and on others, she interrogated her own memories like the prosecutors who had cross-examined her at trial all those years ago. It simply wasn't in her power to know or control whatever judgments her son would ultimately come to. Only wished he could see that she had tried her best with what she had, that what she had simply wasn't adequate. There was no intention to kill his father. It was just how the gavel struck the wood. She said, "I know we've been through this before, but I am sorry, you know, for everything. I didn't mean for it to happen the way it did."

Orestes reached behind her head and adjusted her pillow. He kissed her on the forehead. She'd been sleepwalking when she committed the action that would commit her—first to an institution and then to the daily task of mortifying herself with memories in front of her forgotten son. He was the one who found her incoherent all those years ago, eyes half-opened and rolling back and forth like something out of a horror movie, bloody knife still in her hand. He had to sweep her off her feet with his leg to avoid becoming a second victim. She'd cratered upon falling to the ground, upon awakening. He remembered her sobs being almost as violent as the stabbing itself. But after the last tear had fallen, she surrendered to a confused and dejected silence, one she would maintain up to and, aside from her short testimony, against her lawyer's advice, through the rest of the trial.

Orestes testified too, on her behalf, to her somnambulant state. He was a witness despite his deep desire to be the judge and jury, despite how much his father had meant to him—a man who unlike most fathers was not only lovable but also likable, the two sharing ballgames and trips to the museums and lunches at Niko Niko's, their favorite Mediterranean cafe on Montrose, in other words, Orestes never had the Oedipal urge he saw in so many others of his peers, which made all those whispers of accusations of betrayal that much more haunting, how his father's ghost had perpetually bombarded his inner eardrum. But none of this was really about his father, and he wouldn't let her make it be about that, not now. Even if it still felt like yesterday, he knew the death wasn't the part he was supposed to be angry about, not anymore. This was about him and her now.

He wanted to say, "How do you still not get it? I can't let go of how you left me. How you refused the help, how you wouldn't get better. Has nothing to do with him."

Said instead, "I've forgiven you for the *murder*, if that's what you're getting at."

She broke the gaze when he said it. It was a fractal conversation, she thought, how it'd always taken a self-similar shape to the last one, both re-opening the wound and then avoiding the heart of the matter, each singular iteration a miniature version connected to the ongoing larger conversation they lived inside, only recognizable in the curves of the boundary lines they drew, which were stuck inside an even larger conversation between mothers and sons dating back to prehistoric humans, every repetition a self-affine form connecting, through symmetry, what they *meant* and couldn't *say* to what they *said* and couldn't *mean*, and what it all meant and said about the rest of us too.

She wanted to respond. "I know it felt like a *murder*, and I'm sure that even without being *guilty* in the law's eyes, I'm as *guilty* as *sin* to you, however it is you define either of those words. I'm not asking for a clean slate, but I promise you I've spent so much time running through that night, over and over again, seeing if there were anything that could have snapped me out of it, anything I could have done differently. But look at me now, don't you think I've had…," had she said it, she would have unwrapped one of the bandages part way and showed him the flesh purpling into black on her forearm, before adding, "…plenty enough suffering for one lifetime? Not like I got out unscathed. Would you just understand that none of this was easy for me? That I lost someone I loved too. That I have to live with the guilt. That I didn't do any of it *to you*."

Instead, she changed subjects. It had been a pipe dream to think they could talk it out on her death bed. She'd read too many books about dying, which could only ever be theories about dying and said nothing of dying in and of itself. Her expectations didn't match this new reality. She asked. "Sorry. There's no need to discuss it, not now, why don't you just tell me a story instead?"

"A story?" His repetition of her question was partly meant to stall and partly just confusion at the request. He often considered himself a storyteller, with the way he played the guitar, his rare form of synesthesia, the notes like plot moves he could literally see and hear at the same time inside his head, his ability to access on stage what he assumed was some tiny piece of the collective unconscious, to bring it back front and center, a little piece of something to help the people, to sweep them away in hypnotic heroic movements, to take listeners on quests for scales of harmonious magnitude. In other words, his guitar played epic inspired by a visionary sonic muse. But he wasn't an oral storyteller.

"You used to tell me the best stories when you were a boy. You lived to entertain me." She spoke slowly, enunciating every syllable through raspy breath, the pain in her bones chattering through her teeth.

"Sorry, Dawn." He said her first name rather than call her mom out of an intended habit he'd honed to remind the both of them. "Don't really remember much from my childhood. The last shrink said it was probably a protection mechanism..." He saw her flinch when he said it, "...but that's off-topic—can't trust my shrink even if it were good for me to—anyway, I can't think of a story off the top of my head. Why don't you tell me one of those stories I told you as a child? Help jog my memory." Her legs shivered underneath her blanket. He added, "That is, if you can."

She took another slug from the cup. Looked at him. Breathed heavy. "Sure, why not? Not like the pain will kill me any faster than the painkillers." She laughed and started coughing again. Then she settled herself. "Why don't you give me a cigarette first? That is, if you don't mind me smoking." She smiled a smile that couldn't really smile. Eleanor Rigby started to play out of the speaker. She said, "Oooh, my favorite." When she opened her mouth to sing about lonely people, Orestes zeroed in on her repulsive brown and yellow teeth, he couldn't get used to them, were like a goblin's. What happened to the young woman he used to call Mom?

What happened to her little boy?

He reached into his blue jeans. Pulled out a pack of Pall Mall Blue Shorts, took a filter king out, placed it between her lips, then pulled out a lighter from the same pocket and offered her a flame. Got up and walked to his desk, which was squeezed in the corner of the room behind the side of the bed, underneath a floor lamp. He opened the desk drawer and retrieved an ashtray.

He remembered when she'd moved in after being released from the Mandelbrot Hospital [for the Criminally Insane]—they'd taken the latter half of the name off of the sign in the 1990s, but it was still run by the Texas Department of Corrections in Galveston. She could have been picked up from that hospital so much sooner, the terms of her not-guilty verdict by reason of insanity meant they'd only hold her until they could be assured she wouldn't be a danger to herself or others, which ended up being a lot longer than anyone had really bargained for. She wouldn't talk to the doctors, wouldn't go to sleep in the room they'd set up to observe her dreaming patterns, she'd sometimes slap or scratch the orderlies and guards, refusing to take any medication—a game of chicken that went on for nearly twenty years. Even her release wasn't because they felt like her mental health was any better. It was simply too expensive to keep housing an aging inmate with physical health problems that were worse than the mental ones that had landed her there in the first place.

Orestes placed the ashtray on the tray-table next to the cup. It wasn't so much that he wanted his old life back, all those nightly parties in this same room after the bar had closed down—he was even halfway grateful that the nuisance of her presence had forced him out of some of his bad habits—but he didn't want this life either, and he didn't want whatever tonight was going to lead to. He sat back down on the edge of the bed by his mother's feet. Watched her take another sip of her drink. Everything already set in motion. He lit a cigarette of his own. Took quick puffs, like it was a race.

She inhaled slowly, exhaled slower, and said, "Damn that's good."

"At least something is." He said it reflexively, as if he'd

momentarily forgotten that her impending meeting with Thanatos on the River Styx must have had just as heavy an emotional effect on her. His mother the classical scholar and he who couldn't help but follow in her toeless footsteps, the lost respect making no difference. She seemed to ignore the comment.

"So you want a story of me getting told a story by you?" She guided them back to the exercise at hand, the thing that might get them through it somehow, this most awkward interaction in a whole lifetime full of awkward interactions. At least this one wasn't monitored by a prison guard posing as a nurse. She reached her hand to her chin and rubbed it with her decrepit half-digits. "There was this time when you were maybe four or five, and your father and I took you camping at Lake Livingston, do you remember that?"

"I don't know."

"Well, you know how your father was, all that back to nature talk he always liked to spout. I think we went to celebrate the end of a legislative session, the Great Outdoors, he kept saying. Chance to get away. I had only hoped I packed enough bug spray. Your father took you down to the lake while I put burgers on the grill. When they were done, you still weren't back, so I sat down to read and waited. I was lost inside a volume of Ishmael Reed if I remember correctly, because it was during that time I had been going to conferences with a paper about neoclassicism in postmodernism, Reed's work introduced the specter of African classicism which showed the erasure of half the globe's version of classicism from the rest of academia's research on the period. Anyway, I was making pretty big waves for my career then and feeling conflicted because I wanted to spend more time with you, so when you came running full steam ahead out of the woods and back into the campsite looking for me, yelling and laughing the whole way, when you jumped into my lap, when you gave me a big hug, I put down the book I'd just picked up and knew I would choose you over my career forever. Oh, my little Norm, you were so sweet."

Orestes raised his eyebrows, always hated that name, sounded too much like he was supposed to follow a rule. Dawn noticed and stopped for a second. "I'm sorry, still takes a little getting used to, you were Norm back then. What a name you've chosen, though, Orestes." She couldn't help but roll her eyes, the hero he emulated with his very existence, what that meant about her. She shook her head like she was trying to get something out of her ear canal, trying to avoid losing balance by traveling back *there*. He looked on in waiting.

She took a breath that tried to be deep but wasn't deep enough and continued. "Okay, so you told me you saw aliens on the lake, that they came and took you away in their spaceship, that you played these weird games like dominoes and that they fed you light and it was yummy like guacamole. You were detailed about it, descriptive, was striking for a little boy to say how he felt, how he remembered, all so clearly. You were always smart, you know, the smartest person I've ever met—but, I'm your mother, so I guess I would say that. You told me they asked you to bring me to them. I followed you down the short path through the trees to the lake. You started waving and pointing. Kept saying, 'Do you see them, Mommy?' I didn't see anything, though, nothing at all. Yet there was something so much more than overactive imagination happening in you, I was sure you could actually see something, I'd seen you when you were pretending, and this was not one of those times. I've often wondered about what happens to perception when our brains grow out of childhood, like I remember being a child with a world of wonder, but the essence of childhood, the true feeling, that way of seeing everything as new and magical, well I guess *gone* would be the most precise word for it. It was *gone*. I couldn't help but feel envious of you. I know it sounds crazy, but you were looking into some separate dimension, you must have been,

14

some alternate reality, I'm sure of it, was a real experience somehow, and I just didn't have access to it. I wanted access, I wanted it so bad, it seemed like you had actually swallowed light, some alien form of love embodied. Whether it had come from outer space or just inside your own head didn't matter, it changed you for the better. We went back to the campsite, ate dinner, and then made s'mores, you sat in my lap some more and kept telling me it was going to be okay, like all of a sudden I was the child and you were the parent. But maybe I saw it and missed it, because I had no frame of reference. Or maybe it's still to come. Maybe you were looking into the future. Hopefully, it'll come. Better come soon."

She looked confused all of a sudden, like she'd forgotten where she was going, where she would end up, what they were supposed to take away. She took another slug from her drink.

He said, "Aliens, huh? Well I did like fantasizing about monsters when I was a kid." It was like he hadn't even heard her. He got up from the bed, put out his cigarette, which was still only half-smoked, and looked at his watch. "I should load up now."

She watched him walk into the bedroom and heard him open the closet. There was shuffling and clunking and zipping and more clunking. In the two years she'd been on *the outside*, not one time could she get him to stay with her for more than five minutes before he left the room or changed the topic. Tonight would be no different, despite her needing it to be, despite her long-held belief that all things should end differently than they continue. She understood that he hadn't wanted her to move in here, that this was an ultimate sacrifice on his part, but it would all be over with soon, and it was her last chance to get anything like closure. Could he at least allow her that? He was still a stranger, this man who had once been something like her son.

To his credit, he had taken care of her, when she, admittedly, had lost the will to take care of herself, and then, yes, he'd agreed to help her when she moved in, even after everything, and then he'd agreed to help her again when she wanted to end it, despite her condition not truly being *terminal*, could have gotten a few more years out of this wretched life if she'd wanted to, if only there was still a place for her in it. It made sense to both of them in their own ways, what they were doing here tonight, but she needed it to make sense to him in the way it made sense to her, even if that was a technical impossibility, and even if she wasn't sure why she needed it.

Her son, now Orestes, going so far as to make it legal on his driver's license, to make it real with his art, what his life's work meant, the thing he needed to become a man, to put *The End* on the ending, he would serve her the lethal cocktail, commit matricide, she knew he wanted it, even if he didn't know that he wanted it, to put in the last piece of the jigsaw puzzle, the last line to this myth they'd chosen to reiterate, to weave with the very fabric of their lives. She was giving that to him tonight, requesting the deed for herself when he wouldn't take it upon himself. She only wanted a little assurance in return.

In the bedroom, Orestes double checked his guitar case for an extra pack of strings. He might break one if the tension on the tuning keys got overturned. The Fender Heavy Duty Strings were too crucial to his identity to ever be caught without a backup. It might take more effort when holding cords, but there was no other gauge that would match his rage so perfectly when the distortion hit the breadth of the excesses of coiled steel, when the plot moves on his synesthesiatic soundscape tended toward apocalypse, when the dissonance within which he could pitch his dark fantasies flew out of his amplifier like bottle rockets and rained down freedom on the unknowingly enslaved revolutionaries that make up any kind of a crowd, those boys becoming men and those men remaining boys, all unified by the fists they threw in the air for causes they knew little about. As he sat there and thought about playing the show tonight at the same time that Dawn would be passing on, Orestes realized how all his desires (especially the worst ones) would one day be realized.

His mother made the realization of this particular one harder by only her presence in his home, like he knew she was perfectly well aware what the names he had chosen for himself and for his band signified about his wish for her to be out of his life permanently, including his mental life, at least, it was a desire he'd had for a long time, but it was a desire that had also dissipated, and he didn't know if she knew that. Caretaking had made Orestes' hatred just a little bit easier to stomach, the endless repetitions of applying this ointment and giving that pill and sticking in that needle all forming a faux-reconciliation, an extra coat of emotional armor, provided the two continue not to talk to each other too much, which was usually pretty easy to do since Dawn was often too tired to stay awake (even if she was also generally in too much pain to fall asleep). He would not admit to her that he'd even halfway enjoyed having her here, that it didn't exactly make him come to terms with the self-destruction his life had turned into after she'd destroyed it first, but it gave him a chance to see what coming to terms might have looked like.

His silence meant the concept of his conceptual doom metal band would go on, his vengeance, with or without his continued intention behind it. As an artist, it probably meant growth and change, maybe even in his personal life too, now more than ever, there was no choice but to forge ahead. He was happy they had chosen the night before he departed for tour as the night they would do it, a change of setting would serve him well. He zipped his guitar case back up and slung it across his back, then he grabbed his suitcase for the road and set it on top of his amplifier, which consisted of an 800 watt Marshall head on top of a four-by-ten cabinet with wheels on the bottom. He pushed the amplifier out of the bedroom, back past his mother. Thought he saw tears in her eyes. She looked like she wanted to say something. He stopped rolling the amp, pulled his guitar back off of his shoulder and leaned it up against the wall. He came to her bedside and stood above her, looking down.

Dawn returned his gaze. She shook her cup, feeling it tap against the phantom limbs of her ring finger and pinky, the nerve damage a result of gangrene from Dawn not managing her blood sugar and not telling anyone about it, could have stopped the progress of the disease if she'd spoken up when the digits were merely a rosy red in the mornings, in any case, she'd almost died after they'd purpled, after it spread to her forearms, during the short diabetic coma she'd gone into. It had changed her life as much as going to prison had, in that same revolutionary way, all routines upended, new relationships for everyone involved. She held out the cup and asked her son. "Will you top this back off with a little more whiskey? It's getting watered down."

He walked back into the kitchen and poured more bourbon in her drink, which was only half drunk. He wondered if she'd already had enough. When he came back out, he asked, "Did I tell you I ran into Craig and Izzy this morning?" The gay couple that lived upstairs. Orestes' favorite people in the complex. Kept fresh flowers out along the walkways without being asked or paid to do it. Always came by to visit with Dawn and relieve some of his stress. Had even encouraged him to go on tour when he second guessed himself, them probably assuming he was guilty leaving her for two weeks. "I reminded them about taking care of you while I'm on tour."

"Good idea. My corpse could use some company."

"Sorry. Just going over the plan." It wasn't that he'd forgotten about what they were doing, not completely.

"Relax. Everyone will just think I died of disease. Probably won't even do an autopsy unless you ask for one."

"You're right." Orestes stood again. He wondered if

Dawn had thought about if she had a soul, and if it might go somewhere after, and where she thought it might. She'd raised him Methodist, but it was only really by name. They did church on Easter and Christmas and the rest of the year they stayed home. Basically, he'd never really given a whole lot of thought to religion, not even after his father died. But now with his mother's end so close, he couldn't help but focus on what might be up there, or out there. Was harder to continue not to believe. He felt like he should leave her with what time she had left to make whatever reconciliations she wanted to make with God or the universe or whatever it was—the afterlife, if that's where she was going, it would be upon her soon. He hoped his helping her find it didn't influence his own standing in the afterlife, if there were even such a thing.

Dawn was more focused on the little bit of time she had left. She didn't want him to leave yet, but she didn't know what else to say to keep him there. He walked up and kissed her forehead again. She could only get out, "I love you."

He felt backed into a corner. The kiss on the forehead didn't require an acknowledgment of what wasn't a lie but what they knew to be true and maybe not deserved, even in the midst of her last few breaths. Now he was forced to put words behind it, if he didn't want to regret not saying it back.

"I love you too, Mom."

He picked up his guitar and slung it across his shoulder, opened the door, maneuvered the front wheels of his amp over the threshold, then pulled the other two over keeping the suitcase balanced on top. He shut the door behind him, remembering to remember the last time he'd ever laid eyes on the life that had given him this half-life.

After soundcheck, Orestes walked down from the stage area upstairs and sat down behind the taps at the downstairs bar in

Rudyard's British Pub. The regulars called it Rudz for short, and the super-regulars called it Montrose's Living Room for the way it created a sense of family out of the old queens, punk rockers, metalheads, avant-garde artist types, drug dealers, hipsters, tournament dart players, and pinball enthusiasts who all called the *gayborhood* home. The atmosphere felt more and more dysfunctional the older Orestes got.

He wore his greasy black hair in front of his face so that no one would see him—not right away—except for maybe Patti, the bartender, who he needed to see him. He looked up from his stool at the empty Jaegermeister bottles lining the shelf above the bar, the only evidence left to all those debauched evenings. This playground for the types of people who grew up too fast to never get old. When Patti walked down from the other end of the multi-colored ceramic-tiled bar, he nodded at her. Without any showing of recognition (as per usual), she walked to the cooler behind the bar and grabbed a Lone Star Tallboy, then sidled over to the freezer, pulled the Jaeger out, and poured a shot into one of the shot glasses just out of the dishwasher. It was a routine they'd practiced to perfection over the decade she'd worked there. She set the round down in front of him and said, "O, honey, how you doing tonight? Hear you're going out on tour again."

"Yeah, going on tour."

The idea had grown on him, but truthfully, Athena, their singer, had to demand it at first. The last time they'd been out, they'd only made enough money to cover gas, barely broke even for the whole damn tour. Orestes had broken a lease to go, not being able to pay both the rent and the costs of travel. When they returned, he had to stay with Nestor, the drummer, old windbag that he was, a whole month on sagging couch cushions, it felt more like six months with all the nev-er-ever-ever-ending stories Nestor always kept him up past midnight to tell. Of course, now that his mother was maybe taking her last breath inside his current home while he took his first drink at his second home, maybe getting stuck some-where else again for just a little while might be a good thing.

Patti, using her bartender's sixth sense, reassured him. "You'll be great. You should play more anyway. No one plays the guitar like you do. You take people places."

"Right? I keep telling this guy." He heard Chico behind him. Felt a slap on his shoulder. "O, what's up man? Going on tour again, huh?"

Orestes wished the band hadn't flyered the event tonight as a tour kickoff party. He'd be having some version of this conversation all night long. He hung his head down further. Chico extended his hand to right under Orestes' nose. He had to contort his arm to meet Chico's wrists with his own hand. "Gonna give it a whirl," he said, doing some sort of shake-snap-fist-bump thing with the tattooed knuckles on the receiving end that said *PAIN.*

Orestes scooted back in his swiveling chair closer to the bar. Chico moved in. He said. "No shit. Been a while, hasn't it?"

Orestes moved back again. "Let's see," he paused, also thinking backwards, which led him to think about Dawn. "At least five years."

Chico moved in some more. "Nice. When you leaving?"

Orestes stood up and used his back as a barrier as he looked over his shoulder. He leaned forward onto the bar. "After the show tonight. Heading to Austin. Got an afternoon show at Mohawk tomorrow for a local radio station. Bunch of folks following along if you want to take the party on the road."

Patti interrupted. "No shit. I might go with y'all. I'm off tomorrow. You still be here at closing time?"

Orestes said, "I don't see why I wouldn't be. Won't be done with the set till around last call."

Chico said, "Sorry, man. I can't go. Gotta work. Fucking child support." He rolled his eyes when he said it. "You know how it is."

Orestes didn't but he nodded in faux-empathy, relieved that Chico had turned him down. He didn't want him there with the band, not really. Chico wasn't a real friend even if the two would refer to each other that way out of the obligation of their common membership in an underground community. But Chico was more of a B-movie character than a real person, if there were even a distinction these days, everyone seemed to be imitating some kind of fiction. Orestes most of all, who had chosen to conform to a story that was the summer blockbuster of its own day, in ancient Athens, only considered high brow now because of all the empires it had survived through. Sometimes he thought it made him somehow more noble that he was out in the open about it. In any case, he didn't trust Chico as far as he could throw him, partly because of his profession.

"Speaking of work, I'm putting some in right now. You need anything tonight? I got you man." Chico held his finger to his nose and took a couple of quick sniffs, as if Orestes wouldn't know what he was talking about before he was even talking about it, but Orestes was trying to avoid what Chico was selling tonight, as futile as that effort might turn out to be. Chico either didn't notice or didn't care. "I'm donating ten percent of my take to Damon's family."

Cocaine for a good cause. Orestes almost laughed. It wasn't about Damon. Damon's story was sad, he'd had a stroke two weeks ago, was only forty-three, another local musician, the drummer for Tom Pain and the Revolution, had been in all sorts of hometown bands over the years, was a legend of sorts. Never had a real job to speak of. The hospital was sure to bankrupt him if it hadn't already, and not just monetarily. The doctors weren't particularly optimistic about a full recovery, which is why his band members had set up a Go Fund Me to replace the insurance he didn't have—to help his family, who would be taking care of him the rest of his life, whether that was two weeks long or two decades. It was the third Go Fund Me Orestes had donated to for sick musicians this year, even though he didn't make enough money to take himself to the doctor. All these guys in the scene weren't getting any younger—he wanted to do his part while there was time—the donations would only last as long as the sympathy did. They were doing a benefit for Damon tonight, in addition to the kickoff party for the Libation Bearers. Rudz was giving the door to his family. Orestes hoped someone would do a benefit for him someday when he needed it, which he often feared would be sooner rather than later.

"So, you want anything or what?" Chico said again. Ever the tempter, ever showing up at the wrong time. Maybe Orestes would stroke out tonight, would be poetic with Dawn going down at home and all. But he really was trying to stop. He'd made it a month since the last time. Wouldn't back down yet, he thought, while also hearing the hamster start running on the squeaking wheel inside of his head—*screech, screech, screech*. He'd ignore it as long as he could. "Not right now, man. Let me get a few drinks in me first. Hey, Patti, grab me another round."

He took his shot and slammed down half of his first beer. Patti set the next two drinks in front of him. He slammed the second half and handed her the empty. Then took a still large but not quite as big gulp of his second full beer. It'd been a while since he'd started off this quickly. He'd wondered again if enough time had passed—*screech, screech, screech*—if Dawn was still breathing or not.

Chico looked at Patti and pointed to Orestes' shot. "Say, let me get one of those. And I'll get his."

"Thanks."

Truthfully, Orestes hated it when people bought him shots, since it always presumed a shot in return. The mental scorecards were exhausting. But Patti walked away and was back before he'd had the time to continue to brood over what was a minor predicament. Chico held up a toast.

"See you in the emergency room."

"See you in the emergency room."

They clinked glasses—*screech, screech, screech*—then tapped their shots to the bar before tossing them back. Orestes looked at all the patches on Chico's denim vest, skulls and strippers and drug paraphernalia in almost all of the band logos. The whole bullshit, die young, don't give a fuck attitude they'd all adopted in their youth had faded and stretched like their tattoos into their now older skin. But they were still young enough to go too early, and Orestes wasn't really about the slow suicide anymore, even if he couldn't help himself some nights—*screech, screech, screech*. He looked at Chico. "Fuck it, might as well, you got a G?"

"Yeah, man, I got you. Meet me in the bathroom."

Orestes walked with a little lean in his step. No matter the horrible guilt he felt every single time he bought drugs now, there was also a built-in excitement to it, part of which was getting to feel like a gangster he had no business feeling like, which was maybe why his appropriated gangster lean looked more like a pirate's peg-leg hop. Chico met him in a stall a couple minutes later. Handed him a bag inside of a handshake. Orestes passed a wad of cash from his own end. He did two bumps after Chico walked out, then flushed the toilet in case anyone was listening, walked to the sink, ran cool water, held his fingertips under the stream, then took some droplets and snorted them up his nose to soothe the rusty canals. He breathed deep, hardly felt like anything, the cocaine from his heyday was better, or maybe he was just more into it. He thought about flushing the bag back down the toilet but knew that he wouldn't. He wished it were some other way, but progress came slow, if you could call it progress. But it wasn't that he couldn't say he'd made no progress, that wouldn't be exactly true either. He certainly felt like being a binger was better than being a daily user, which he used to be. Now, it was mostly on the weekends, with an occasional weekday or two in between, sometimes even managing to be *good* for a month or more, like the last month up until tonight, but he would have to remind himself of the *responsible* version of himself tomorrow, would have to promise to himself all over again that he wouldn't get sucked in again, that tonight he was just getting it out of his system, one last time after the last last time. There was still hope, even if it was a hope that contributed to his drug (kind-of-still-a-) problem, a hope that the world could be some way it hadn't proven to be yet.

When he came out into the bar from the bathroom, he took a look at the clock on his phone. He needed to make it upstairs. He walked back to the downstairs bar where his beer was sitting with a coaster on top. Took it off and slammed the rest down. He yelled over to Patti who was now down at the other end of the bar. "One more."

She appeared moments later with another beer and another shot. Said, "Putting 'em down fast tonight. You okay?"

It was another part of their bartender-patron relationship routine, the gentle reminders that he might be drinking too much with the assurances that she'd never cut him off as long as he didn't ask for it. "Yeah, I'm fine. Just trying to get *right* before I go onstage."

The Sad Fucks, the openers, were already playing by the time he went upstairs. They were a parody alt-countryish punk band who had crowd favorites like "Even Cowgirls Get HPV" and "Mamas Don't Let Your Babies Grow Up to be Crackheads (Like Me)." The latter song was written by Uncle One-Eyed Willie, their lead guitar player, an autobiographical number, or so the rumors went. In any case, The Sad Fucks played the same set they always did, the same set they'd been perfecting for twenty years, it always provided some sense of reunion, and of communion, the sense of making our past ages golden—no matter if it was pyrite or not.

Orestes once had so much hope in this music scene. When he'd been tagged Best Guitar Player in the *Houston Press* for the first time, when the Libation Bearers had gone on their first tour all those years ago. They'd played their first kick-off party in this very bar. In fact, it was the first time Orestes had been allowed inside. It was before he was legally allowed to drink, they'd drawn huge X's on his hands in permanent marker to let everyone know, which was super embarrassing considering he had always longed to be an adult and didn't want to be recognized as a child after he had already turned the legal age to die for his country, if he had wanted to do such a thing, which he vehemently didn't. He'd gotten drunk even with the symbol of innocence by letting friends sneak him Long Island Teas. They had been celebrating. The band had just signed a developmental deal with Electra records, in part, he was sure, because of his guitar being named Electra. They'd even gotten to open for Metallica for six nights on the Southwestern leg of that same tour, on the Libation Bearers' way to Los Angeles, where they were moving. Seemed so sure that it would happen, that dropping out of high school had been a wise decision, had given him a head start.

When the Libation Bearers went to Mexico for the first time, they'd found they had developed an even bigger following than stateside. Kept having to reschedule the dates for bigger venues because the shows were selling out so quickly. South America had been no different. They would even fill a couple of stadiums as the headliners. But when they got back to Los Angeles, Orestes, who had developed quite the cocaine problem south of the border, caught a felony possession charge for a couple of grams he had on him while driving drunk. The sales of their first album, *Agamemnon's Revenge*, had done okay but not well enough for the label to put up with the headache. The Libation Bearers got dropped. Wasn't long before they were back in Houston. A few more tours south of the border, where he'd made only enough money to develop a more worrisome drug habit, and then they'd just turned into mostly a local thing, washed out, has-beens.

He watched the Sad Fucks play one of their faster numbers, "Bloody Asshole Morning." Felt something, would he call it guilt? Like sure there was a time when this whole thing was fun, the sadistic lyrics only words, how they couldn't hurt you. He still dug the energy, but he wasn't so much into the mythos of rock and roll anymore, he thought, while he walked over to the upstairs bar. His beer and shot were already on the counter when he arrived. Gutter was working. He yelled over the music, "O! Knock 'em dead tonight."

Had Dawn taken her last breath yet, Orestes thought again. He asked himself if the guilt could facilitate a rationalization for love, were the tears that he wouldn't let fall a form of love? He shook his head and took his shot, tipped his empty glass at Gutter, a gesture of thanks he wasn't sure he meant. Gutter walked over in between songs. He said a little quieter, "Hear you're going on tour?"

This again, Orestes thought. "Yeah, yeah, hitting the road. Can I get another shot?"

Gutter poured another one. Orestes took it. The music kicked back up. Gutter yelled, "This one's on me. Have fun up there. Sell some merch!"

How much fun could you have when you were always running away?

He yelled out a verbal thanks to Gutter as he walked off toward the bathroom to do a couple more bumps, hoping to speed up his fingers while slowing down his brain. Saw the graffiti on the stall door as he stuck his key into the baggie. It said Nazi Punks Fuck Off, a throwback to the Reagan years in these years that felt exponentially more hateful than the Reagan years, even if they probably weren't any more so or less so, was it only because his perspective had changed, or had everyone else changed too? How did we get back here, he thought, as he scooped a bump out of the bag to ward off the hefty amount of alcohol he'd already put down in not even an hour. Took it up his nose, then thought how the phrase *took it up his nose* could be his life's motto, a survival mechanism and a death wish all rolled up in one like two sides of a dollar bill forming an eternally filthy Möbius drug straw.

Dawn struggled to stay awake knowing the blackness would soon be endless. She only wanted a few more moments to see, to remember her boy, blurry as both the seeing and the remembering were. She imagined him playing his guitar, swaying to the rhythm, lilting to the sadness of the moment. She'd never heard her son play with his band before, had never even heard recordings of their work on the radio before. When he played the guitar in his room, he'd keep the practice amplifier turned down so low that she only caught a random note or two escaping under the door frame. Nothing like a melody. She'd never heard him be harmonious.

She remembered her correspondences with Jack, her little brother, rest his soul, who had agreed to take Orestes in when Dawn went to the hospital. "I couldn't tell you how he's doing. His grades are shit, but he won't talk to me about it. He doesn't do much of anything except play the guitar. He's great at that, though. A real original. It's something to be proud of." Coming from Jack, a man with a vinyl collection that necessitated a whole extra room of his house, she knew the praise was deserved.

Orestes looked so confident in the pictures in the frames and on the posters on his walls, in his trademark leather vest, Electra, his guitar, wrapped around his shoulders like an orphaned sibling. Oh, how they'd cry together, a wail in E flat, because Dawn could hear it now, even though she'd never heard it before, he was playing her swan song, a lifetime of practice, of repetition, of preparation, of writing and rewriting and then practicing and then practicing some more, all for this very moment, this moment when they'd say goodbye together in spirit. She was sure she was hearing the notes he was playing right now where he was onstage at Rudz, in a separate building sharing a sonic quantum entanglement with the living room where she lay dying. But she could hear the story he could hear, and it was still bringing life, as temporarily as all life is brought. The story he had created for them, the story that ended just as adulthood was supposed to begin, a life that continued on as the loss of a life, in the only form that could hold it, in a musical composition so vital it spoke best to the dead. Was she dead yet? She wondered.

Not quite, she thought again, as she opened her eyes to a blurry vibration of equalizing light. She picked up the sippie cup, forgetting it was empty, wished Orestes were here to open the lid, wished she could suck on the whiskey and morphine soaked ice. It occurred to her that she might be more in love with the idea of dying than death itself, with the idea of becoming one with her son in spirit more than the idea of leaving her body behind. It was all good, though, so long as she could keep hearing the music, she wanted more of the music. If she could only keep her mind numbingly alive a few more minutes, she could keep channeling this mystical umbilical cord, this bi-location of sound.

The guitar work was hauntingly beautiful in a raw and aggressive sort of a way, oh what fury, the pinnacle, the solo, *the hammers, the finger taps, the string bends, the whammy bar, the chorus pedal*, the words flowing in like strange new harmonies, words she never used before, words she shouldn't have understood, words she knew intuitively because they came from the river that ran underneath his skin, flowing like the techniques he used to make his notes resonate, yes, he was a man of technique, yes, he was a man, he was a man now, would be more of a man in just a few more minutes.

She looked back at the pictures on the wall, the one where Orestes was standing next to a Virgin of Guadalupe statuette in a roadside dilapidated prayer temple, candles lit all around him. Stood in front of a papier-maché mask hanging on a nail on the wall just over his shoulder, a skull wearing a crown with a rose in its mouth, a caption underneath the picture read, *La Gira por la Murete, 2001, Mexico City.* He was smiling, looked happy, in fact, this was a picture she'd returned to often on all those lonely days in the living room by herself, the smile an absent host. She liked to think he might one day be happy again.

She didn't want him to hate her. Figured if she could hear the sound, then maybe he could make out her intentions on the other end. Could come to terms with what she did to his father, with how it had actually happened. True, she might have wanted out of being a wife, might have wanted out of motherhood, might have even wanted out of womanhood, but she knew she loved Orestes and his father. She hoped Orestes could figure out what she never could, or, at least, she hoped he could find a way to blend the never-ending chaos into a proper quodlibet.

She thought of her own mother, Maggie. How she'd graduated from college at nineteen, in just four semesters, with a double major in education and journalism. How she'd married because it was expected, taught high school because it was expected, kept holding out hope that her journalism degree might come in handy after others had blazed the trail. Dawn had trouble then realizing the courage it took to even major in journalism at a time when women were only allowed to nurse the sick and teach the young. She remembered how she used to call her mom a sellout.

But Dawn really hated her mother when she became her, when she became an English major for lack of any conviction that any higher ambitions would pay off. Of course, Dawn did love stories, that part was true, but she didn't feel satisfied when she graduated from Tulane *summa cum laude,* when she felt hopeless about the job market and retroactively wished for a more practical major, when she applied to the PhD program at Rice University. They were impressed with her writing sample, about using fractal logic to evaluate western classical narrative, about how stories formed the perceptive outline of a shape we use over and over again to practice our judgments, as we move forward into more and more depth. She had gotten the idea when thinking about her newlywed husband, who happened to share his name with a famous mathematician, there was no relation either of them knew of, but when she'd seen the shape of the von Koch curve, she thought, that's the logic of the Odyssey, not a series of concentric circles like some scholars propose, but anyway, she also thought that if she were a real academic, she'd have been studying the fractal effects of algorithms on the global economy, and how to dismantle such algorithms to make life better for more people, as far as it went, she became just another version of Maggie, her mother, consigned to a classroom for the rest of her life pretending to save the world one kid at a time without copping to the fact that more often than not she was credentialing more Future Psychopaths of America for careers in politics and business than she ever was truly training young people how to critically think to solve the problems of tomorrow that their generation would face, which just so happened to be mostly the same problems every generation faces, just taking on new shapes as they progressed through time more than any solutions ever did. Maybe that was why she really hated herself for her profession?

Of course, the more important question to her was why did she hate herself for wanting to have a family? Because she did want to have a family by the time she had her doctorate. Elliot, her husband, was working as a speech writer for Ann Richards, and she was offered a tenure track job at the University of Houston after five long years of working as an adjunct. They didn't have all the money in the world at that point, but they both had careers that were budding. They had relative stability. It was her late twenties, and her maternal clock was ticking louder than it ever had before.

But she also didn't want to be known as the type of woman who puts her family before herself. And then she ended up being that type of woman anyway, whatever it means to be a type of a woman, or a woman itself, for that matter. Because that was really the problem, why she hated her mother, why she hated herself more, this pressure to fit into subcategories of subcategories of subcategories in a taxonomy that had no common ancestor short of the oppression which housed it inside of borders with no landmarks or fences, which she also always felt left outside of in ways that left her feeling inwardly disfigured.

Dawn started bawling uncontrollably as she heard Orestes' song work into the final breakdown section. She picked up the sippie cup again and put it to her lips, if she just kept trying, there would be more medicine inside. When she found it empty, she tried to throw it against the wall but it only made it to her feet. It exploded like a piñata, candy fell from the sky, she held out her tongue, the room shook. Her blurred vision turned into a prism, and the sound of Orestes' guitar ringing out at the end of a song enclosed her inside of an invisible womb. She said her last prayers to herself even if she addressed them to a higher power, *God, if you are out there, I don't know how this forgiveness thing works, but I might want some of that.* Her eyes drooped. The temperature in the room reached a rolling boil. Her head fell back and her breath stopped in a mid-thought that was also a last thought, something having to do with being saved. With trying to save her son.

Orestes played a Phrygian dominant scale, galloping down the fretboard, his digits playing the role of the four horsemen on an apocalyptic left hand. He looked out into the crowd like it was a jury standing in judgment, holding the fury of a life poorly lived within the chaotic mental balance that coincides with making any important decision. His waiting fate was slamming into the kids in the mosh pit who were slamming into each other. These lonely, anti-social, mostly white kids, not quite his peers anymore, but looking like some new version of his peers who harkened back to his actual peers fifteen years ago, all throwing middle fingers in the air, giving each other the kinds of physical bruises that matched the mental ones a polite society had already doled out to them. Freaks, nerds, weirdos, geeks, rejects. The ones who got sick of quietly taking it, who started making noise to fight back, even if they never considered how polite society had constructed a whole set of soundproofing intentionally designed to filter out their noise.

But most of these kids had shitty bands, wanted to be on stage. Some would eventually figure out the magic, those who paid attention, those who studied Orestes' finger positions, those who emulated him like a hero. But hero worship was the whole problem, the thing they hadn't figured out yet, how this unceasing desire to be center stage will eat you alive, how it can only ever make your own pain more real than anyone else's. All these kids who would lay some kind of claim to manifest destiny on the very idea of struggle, which was all storytelling ever really was when trapped inside a commodity culture.

Orestes thought again about his own role as a storyteller, as he switched into the detective fiction story by pulling on his whammy bar. The tone didn't match Athena's lyrical content, and it wasn't supposed to. "Stand down for the clowns. Let the fools make their rounds." Orestes wished the crowd would stand up for something more than just rock music. The only way out of being a fool was to run around in concentric circles until you're dizzy with something like knowledge, which in the end, always turns into doubt. But the contradiction was part of the act. He needed enough tension on both sides of the issue to make them to feel the tale in their still healthy bones, whether they could hear its literal rattle or not, how an A to a B flat sounded like a crime scene clue and how a C to a D took on the nature of a confession. How a resounding G played through a chorus pedal sounded like the crisis fading into denouement where the genius puts together what everyone else had only been guessing at. Maybe the crowd didn't translate the sound the way he did, through the synesthesia, but he knew they could feel it somehow, the emotional arc like a foundation for a call to action. A freedom to act housed inside his calloused fingertips.

The detective fiction faded out, and Orestes switched into a western number, which on his guitar had a sonic genre more akin to progressive jazz played through a distortion pedal. But the story was about cowboys, how their bodies age. He looked past the slamming kids to the tables behind the standing area, where his actual peers were, men who had learned with age not to stand in judgment and were here more as witnesses, as historians, sipping their beers and nodding their heads slowly, these graying adult teenagers who still wore denim vests with patches, spiked belts, and sunglasses (even while inside). Guys who'd started bands twenty years ago and never came to a place where they could outgrow the identity they'd forged onstage. He could see the good ol' days in the kids in the front, but it was too bad he knew what the rest of their days would look like. He wondered if he could get those kids to turn around and see it too.

Orestes jumped off the monitor and then ran over to the drum riser. Kicked one leg up on top. Nodded his head at Nestor, swayed his hips, watched Athena jump up, pull herself onto the low-hanging rafters and suspend herself from her knees, throwing upside-down devil's locks akimbo. He had to admit it still felt good to be on stage, was part of the reason he couldn't leave this life behind. But maybe he was making excuses, maybe the only way to save those kids was to save himself from the executioner's gaze mirrored in their awe-filled awful faces.

He played his solo while he thought about his own hero, Thunder Perkins, who died of cancer, a destitute man, playing at The Big Easy for tips until he could no longer ride his rickety bicycle with a guitar balanced on his back, his once deep booming voice a raspy parody of itself, lungs wracked from years of smoking both cigarettes and crack. How Thunder was allowed to have the blues, how Orestes would have rather been a blues musician, but he was too white for that. So he played metal instead, which seemed appropriately bleak for his life story based on appropriation, even if it was voided of the soul he hoped he projected.

He switched into the Locrian mode, the mode of the *deus ex machina* for his next solo part, meant to add dissonance over the rest of the band's slow guttural howl. He hit an E flat and felt a bolt of electricity run from his index finger up to his elbow and die in a movement to open D on his dropped tuning. It signified the end of the end. Dawn was gone. Only the stage could protect him from it now. He pulled on his whammy bar again and let Electra wail for him, still being fueled by an adrenaline that hadn't made it real yet.

But he could feel her spirit entering the room like humidity coming in from an open door in the summertime, like the swampland of his home city was no longer being filtered out by the overworked air conditioning system on the upper floor of Rudyard's. He could feel a new kind of pressure, how he was weak all of a sudden, even as his fingers kept flying like eagles. He closed his eyes. He could hear the crowd now, not so much yelling and singing along like they were before, but chanting like monks. When he peeked out again through slit lids, it looked like the wooden walls were bubble wrap. He wanted to pop them.

They popped on their own first. The roof flew off, and the swampy air shot upwards and began to swirl like a tornado. There was another pop, then a screech as the electricity gave out. The crowd stopped chanting, went silent, and dropped to their knees. Some tried to fight that too. This was not what they had paid for.

In the sky, there was a flaming chariot approaching like a jet-plane in a holding cycle. Gently descending, circling as if being placed on top of them by the hand of God himself. Dawn was driving the chariot, or some demon who looked like Dawn, her skin was peeling, her hair frazzled like the bride of Frankenstein. She was inhaling and exhaling a noxious green gas. She wanted to take him with her. He wanted to go. It was a better tour than the one he had planned with his band.

She landed on the stage. He got in. She kissed him, exhaled the gas into his mouth. He breathed it in willingly, realizing as he did that it wasn't her who had been playing the role of the demon. Maybe there was no such thing as demons, only the undead. She looked at him and said, "Let's go."

He nodded before getting in. The crowd watched as the chariot ascended like a rocket ship, flying in the direction of the moon, probably to use its gravity to slingshot its orbit back toward the sun which it would approach until the conflagration made it impossible not to depart.

The crowd watched the take off and prayed out loud that this time would finally be the End of Time. Please God. Please. But there was no answer to their collective appeal, only the fading light in the sky, longing to be consumed by a greater fire.

The Bell Witch Hunter & the Curse
of Jacksonian History

I no longer believe in history, antiquity was remade from
scratch in the 1820s when Andrew Jackson commissioned the
great global project, enlisted his Masonic brethren, formed
an elite conspiracy with populist ends, you see, sounds crazy,
but like for real for real, the first verifiable event happened
when Jackson arrived at John Bell's farm in Tennessee, Bell
had been sighting ghost animals down the barrel of his
musket, shots moving through apparitions without resistance,
without blood, ghost dog in the corn fields, ghost turkey on
a fence post, ghost horse at the haystack, ghost dog again,
this time by the creek, eventually, even weirder things happen,
Bell finds he can't speak on certain days, tongue swollen not
in a medical way but like a ghost cat had it, on uncertain days,
polyphonic voices, all call themselves Kate, come out of the
walls & light fixtures in his otherwise quaint home, different
pitches & intonations & accents arguing & contradicting, Bell
gets spooked enough to ask for help, word spreads across the
state to Jackson, who was not yet president but already a proud
veteran, not scared of anything, says he'll defeat the ghost, put
the fear of God into Kate, *that witch*, heads out to Bell Farm
where he stayed overnight, said later, *rather fight an army of the
savagest savages* (his words, not mine) *than spend one more night on
that creepy old farm*, but he also wants accolades, loves acco-

lades, they're the greatest, keeps mulling the problem over, figures ghosts are traumas & traumas are inflicted by men who make history & sadist that Jackson was, he enjoys inflicting trauma almost as much as he enjoys receiving accolades, figures he can solve Bell's problem by creating productive new problems, his people would love him for it, decides he's going to rewrite history, like all of it, cut the witch out with scissors and whiteout the rest, concept wasn't exactly a new one, most powerful kings attempted it once, at least, according to Andrew Jackson they did, because, you see, he plans an agenda, hires his own staff of writers, they put all new words under all the old titles, use aged paper, wear the book bindings down, replace them on the shelves (e.g. *The Metamorphoses, On the Revolution of the Celestial Spheres, The Kabbalah, Hamlet & so on & on & on*) clandestine style, historians start quoting, soon bogus copies become fixed reality, I could continue, but I don't even know how deep it goes, he canonized white as a blinding light, chased a manifested destiny, you see, a few months after Jackson departed, John Bell swallowed a whole bottle of poison, family said Kate made him do it, Jackson claimed the witch was dead, the people called him a ding-dong & when the church bells rang out in funereal songs, he said, *exceptionalism trumps repetition,* while pallbearers loaded the wooden coffin ever so shakily into the horse-drawn carriage.

Per-C and 'Dusa: A Narrative Representation of a Graphic Epic

by Angela Ames, PhD

"Worlds inside of worlds inside of worlds."—MH

Sometimes the quest for a story becomes so engrossing that the searcher herself becomes the sought after. This is what happened to me when I delved into the story of Per-C, a graffiti artist from Houston, TX, whose last entrance into an erased canon, arguably his masterpiece—a hybrid of painting, drama, dance, and magic, a turbulent moving mural using the sky as canvas, done from a window washing platform hung high atop the ivory-colored walls of the First City Tower sometime around the turn of the millennium[1]—shows the fundamental confusion between the purpose, the aesthetic, and the reception of art in public spaces, which is created through a dialogue with an already confused tradition, in a

---

[1] Or so the urban legend goes. I will treat it as real for now in the hopes of allowing the reader to soon discover how essential its assumed realness necessarily is to the way we interpret the meaning of the story. Whether Per-C actually created an illusion, a real effect, or if the city's memory of Per-C was altered somehow—or if it were some combination of all three—Per-C's spectacle transcends the binary between natural and supernatural (as does the real in general), showing how there is no true distinction between natural and supernatural occurrences, only distinctions in our methods of the interpretation of phenomena. Of course, this type of magical relativity is not a new idea (maybe because nothing is), but it is an idea that seems fairly self-evident in the Per-C story. For further useful analysis on this lack of distinction between the natural's and the supernatural's existence in perceptive spaces, please see:

Sotomayor, Edwin. "The Realness of Magic in the Magically Real Histories of De Salazar." Latin American Philology 23(8), 1993.

misshapen dimension where subjective and objective perspectives co-mingle without restriction. Per-C achieved such a grand effect by creating a literal fun house mirror out of spray-paint, reflecting the ground into the thin pollutant-filled air just below the clouds, portraying a symbolic gathering of women who were representative of the real women standing on the ground. He displayed them naked, without their permission, dancing[2] around a gigantic version of his patented 'Dusa head,[3] with all its attendant slithering snakes extending from her follicles, snapping and hissing, creating a rhythm for her laughter to sing to. For some time before that, Per-C had been painting mini-non-moving-non-auditory versions of 'Dusa all over the city, heads so grotesque and captivating as to enslave viewers in stares so penetrating they'd not relinquish until a team of city workers—consisting of one man who wore a blindfold and body camera to avoid becoming entranced and a handful of others directing the blinded worker through an earpiece by watching the video of his camera while locked

---

2   Here we should note how in the binary between dance and stillness, our notions of object and voyeur, of subject and audience, are also problematized. Per-C's boundless production of simultaneous desire and anxiety provoked an imagined hedonism inside a real stoicism, showing how both might be said to be mutual products of the other and, therefore, thoroughly dependent on each other.

3   I will go further in explaining the history behind 'Dusa, but if you haven't caught on yet, Per-C as an artist's persona is also a representation, an allegorical and biographical self-affine connection to the classical Greek hero Perseus, who possessed and used the decapitated gorgon head of Medusa as a weapon in battle to turn his opponents into hard stone. Most are familiar with the idea of the Medusa, so I won't spend too much time on an exegesis of the classical characters here, but I should say that I do subscribe to Bal's theory that the story of Perseus shows the similarity between decapitation and castration as symbolic functions, cutting off the site of the mind in the woman so that the man's own loss of his phallus might be recognized in his sight upon the severed head. This whole process of mutual recognition reveals the destructive longing in men for a femininity that can no longer be embodied. Thus, Bal argues that it is only through the attempt and failure to control feminine beauty, fury, and horror that man can achieve the courage to act out in violence. For her most comprehensive treatment of this idea, please see:

Bal, Helena. *Hard as Stone: The Collision of Agency and Horror in the Heroic Display of Medusa by Perseus.* Los Angeles, CA: Vintage Classic Criticism, 1975.

safely away inside a specialized audiovisual van—would later come along and buff[4] the work off the side of whatever space Per-C had "violated,"[5] setting the spectators free. It turned out that such spectacles were mere dress rehearsals for his final mural, "'Dusa and the Dancing Ladies."

Once the outline for the gigantic sky 'Dusa was completed, those on the ground outside of the First City Tower became frozen and silent, an eerie stillness overtook all of downtown Houston, a statuesque crowd with necks craned toward the sky watched the artist work, not moving even to itch or scratch, some men drooling on themselves, Per-C furiously spraying away, adding figures to his work, the women who began to see their own likenesses were the most engrossed of all. The quiet brought in a chill, even in the midst of a brutal Texas summer, the wind kicked up and the pressure dropped, and when the temperature reached hypothermic levels, the artwork sparked into a fiery motion. The women in the painting crackled into rhythmic kicks, bouncing on the red-hot balls of their feet, swirling around 'Dusa's head, Per-C shading and touching up all the while, switching

---

4   Buffing is the practice of painting over or pressure washing tags (the backbone of graffiti, the names of the artists) off the sides of buildings, fences, and overpasses. The best description of the ongoing battle between buffer and writer can be found in:

Dose-Tre. *Illegal Art: If These Painted Walls Could Scream.* New York: Penguin, 2012.

5   Houston's own mayor once used this exact language, "The artist violated our city," speaking in an interview about a 'Dusa portrait that appeared on an overpass on I-45 heading north into downtown and brought traffic to a standstill for an entire day and a half. While the mayor's response is rather laughable in the face of how her police department and county jails regularly violate the rights of her own citizens, some of the women who were portrayed in the sky during Per-C's masterpiece also used this same word, "violated," when speaking about the effects of Per-C's aesthetic choices. I bring up this double-meaning of intention now as a way of saying that my ironic usage of violated here is not meant to undercut the struggles of those who actually felt, and continue to feel, they were violated by Per-C, even if my own reaction to his work does not yield this same disgust. However, I also plan not to skirt these issues and will work through them further in the body of the text. For right now, I'll only say I think Per-C's violations can also produce liberation and that these contradictory reactions inherently provoke each other when happening in rapidity in a diverse cultural setting.

between tips[6] to give the lines the right width and the shadows the right depth. 'Dusa laughed and laughed and laughed. It went on like that for what "really did feel like an eternity."[7] Eventually, Per-C leapt off the pulley and lift system holding up the window washing platform and joined his women in the sky, moonwalked across the atmosphere (appeared like he had no bungee cord or safety net),[8] all the while playing a painted too-yellow acrylic trumpet, eventually signing his name in purple, which was being exhaled through the blinding horn. When he began to claim possession, to attach an identity to his craftsmanship, the act of bringing finality to his creation, the 'Dusa stopped laughing and began repeating a question, "What are you looking at? What are you looking at? What are you looking at?" Her tone grew more desperate with each iteration, until she was practically shrieking. Per-C finished his name across the bottom, sprayed out a steady stream of more purple, and let the vapors from the can form a cloud around his body and consume him,[9] just before the artwork itself exploded like fireworks into the sky, releasing all who were on the ground back to their normal routines.

---

6   Spray-paint enthusiasts use specialized tips on their paint cans to achieve specialized effects. Having multiple tips is similar to how a traditional painter uses different brush sizes.

7   As cliché as such an observation might sound, this is exactly how 75% of respondents answered my question about how long they thought the duration might have been. I imagine the actual run time was around a couple of hours.

8   This is perhaps only partially true. Most respondents claim they saw no evidence of Per-C's manipulations in achieving such a Jesus-like effect, that, at worst, he was a master magician who hid his tricks well, and, at best, he was a literal miracle worker, able to tap into forces beyond normal human comprehension. However, for the sake of fidelity, there were a couple of respondents who claim they saw a thin rope attached to a harness on Per-C's backside. I tend to believe the majority, that even if it was a trick, Per-C paid enough attention to detail that he wouldn't fail to remember to hide a tiny piece of rope or wire, but either way, I don't think it necessarily takes away from the ambition, or the result, if he did blow his cover a tiny bit.

9   Because Per-C was never heard from again, some believe he literally disappeared that day, vanishing into an alternate dimension or, like in a Buddhist meditation, he achieved some form of enlightenment and became an essential nothingness.

I believe that despite the fantastical descriptions of almost everyone I spoke to about Per-C, that the creation of his artwork lives on in an absolutely true oral history, whether the content is real or not.[10] I will admit that I can't fully attest to the accuracy of the words that are written here, which are formed by reconstructing a comprehensive and cohesive timeline from the several hundred interviews I conducted with various residents of the city who were in attendance at the event or who offered a second-hand account of someone who was a close friend or relative who had attended the Per-C spectacle. Of course, memory is fallible, especially when a memory becomes so distant[11] and when it becomes collectivized, which always leads to an increasing variation in the main plot, but, by a true story, I don't mean true in the sense of whether or not the event literally happened like it is rendered here (or in any of my individual interview subjects' imaginations). I mean simply that this story is true for the true effects it had on the residents of our community, effects which lead to a whole new understanding of the community itself, all through an equally true process of reconstruction that must necessarily search for a universal meaning inside of particular occurrences. Therefore, while responses by residents spanned the range of responses one could have to any event, I will still attempt to synthesize the different reactions into some kind of a workable structure so that we can get closer to a definition of both what is real and what is true about Per-C.

First, though, we should look at the differences in some

---

10   See Note 1.

11   Although no-one has been able to establish an exact date, it definitely took place before 9/11, because security would have been ramped up at the tower otherwise. They most likely would have stopped to check a kid dressed in all black rolling a dolly full of paint cans through the streets of downtown. Of course, that isn't so important. What is important is that over a decade had passed from when Per-C painted "'Dusa and the Dancing Ladies" and when I began conducting my interviews. As such, this decade-long gap was enough by itself to fudge even central details to our story, with or without all of the nuances of personality that come to bear on the act of interpretation.

of the reactions so that we can come to realize where such reactions share a similar shape. Some responses were mostly positive. Like one woman who spoke of how, until Per-C, her strict Catholic upbringing had permanently riddled her with deep embarrassment and shame when viewing things like romantic love scenes in movies and racy magazine covers and such. She said intellectually she felt her response was too extreme to be triggered by things that while at times taste-less were ultimately benign, but when it would happen, it was always the same effect, she'd just be frozen, wanting to look away but not being able to, like what happened at the specta-cle. She said she came to label such feelings as "the paralysis of morality," and it was Per-C who had freed her by showing her how her feelings couldn't actually harm her. She told me:

> When Per-C opened up that reflection of reality, that il-lusion, that funhouse mirror image, when he made that magic, when we looked into the sky and saw ourselves naked, dancing around the acrylic head of the freshly an-imated 'Dusa, whose soft laugh had built into a hyster-ical crying that maintained a perfect rhythm with the Charlie Parker-esque jazz solos he whistled from that horn while he worked, when we couldn't look away or stop from being looked at, being consumed by the saliva-drenched gaze of all those stone-faced businessmen, with our stretch-marks and cellulite and birthmarks and unshaved re-gions on display for all of downtown Houston to see, I can't speak for the others who were there, but I felt no shame.[12]

This same woman, an attorney, later told me after the event was over, she was able to forgive herself for all those years of self-hatred. It had inspired her to recognize the parts in her personality she'd always considered uninspiring, to ask if she were being truthful in her own representation

---

12 Anonymous, Personal Interview, June 22, 2016.

of herself to the world. Per-C saw in her an inner beauty, one she accessed by confronting her falsely perceived lack of outer beauty in public.[13] It led her to take action. She quit her job at the high-priced international law firm she worked at, divorced her husband, and started her own catering business, finally living a life she could choose for herself.

But not everyone felt so freed by Per-C. Some, in fact, felt a range of emotions they became trapped with (and trapped by). These reviews were scathing, like another woman represented in the sky, who told me that Per-C made her deeply uncomfortable,[14] that the accuracy[15] of the picture only made the effect exponentially more threatening. She told me how she'd file a lawsuit against Per-C if she only knew who he actually was. Then, she spoke of her older sister, who had been raped in college by four members of the football team at a frat party her freshman year. Her sister later dropped out of school and became a bartender, an alcoholic, her relationship with her family strained as a result. All from one moment of trauma, a life sentence to endure while her assailants served a mere collective six month jail sentence for their mutual crime—the one who played lookout didn't even get a day behind bars. She said:

I know that what Per-C did to me wasn't a sniff of what

---

13   This might also be thought of as a process of confronting the universal within the particular, seeing one's own idea of beauty as valid in the place of a societal (read: universal) idea of beauty.

14   See Note 5.

15   By accuracy, I mean the focus of attention on the physical and visual details of his subjects, like birthmarks in the right places, hair the right color, and hips the right width, but this does not imply that Per-C really "knew" who these women were, although many were concerned as to how the parts under their clothes were so similar to reality, like his imagination contained an x-ray vision function.

happened to my sister in college, but I had been forced to serve in the realization of a sexual fantasy, stuck with all those sweaty, libidinous men visually preying on my character, against my will. It was the first time I could sort of understand the extent to which my sister was damaged permanently, because I still haven't gotten over Per-C, all these years later, like it still makes me nauseated. Fuck Per-C.[16]

Other reviews were more mixed, blurring the line between what Per-C's intentions might have been and why those intentions might not matter in the face of actions that could be considered destructive to some. A social activist who runs a yearly summer camp called Our Town for the purposes of providing leadership and diversity training to teenagers told me that, while he wasn't there, from what he had gleaned from those he knew who had been in attendance, he interpreted the message of Per-C's work as a benevolent one. He said he thought Per-C was trying to give us a glimpse at the beauty of normal women while also critiquing the horror that our expectations of them can cause. This was why Per-C left no bruise un-rendered and no scab un-picked[17] in his mural, but the activist also talked about how Per-C's failing was how he didn't account for who might have most needed to see his message, he didn't account for the differences between intent and impact. By using a forum so public, by painting unannounced, and by not gaining consent, he inflicted further

16   Anonymous, Personal Interview, February 27, 2016.

17   A colleague and art scholar at Rice, Monica Proulx, PhD, told me that despite the fantasticality of the magic, the cartoonish nature of 'Dusa, and the fact that the whole mural was swirling and bouncing in mid-air, the rest of the painting was quite realist. She says the realism served as the very ground on which the fantastical could begin to form. This was the central premise of her doctoral dissertation, which was eventually published as a whole book of criticism, and has led a new revolution of critique in the contemporary visual arts field. For more on her perspective on how the real is negatively charged on the positive ground of fantasy, please see her book:

Proulx, Monica. *Murphy's Law in Painting: What Can Be Imagined Can Corrupt The Real.* New York, NY: NYU Press, 2013.

trauma on some members of the community who he might have been trying to help, forcing them to relive the loss of agency they had already suffered long ago.

The activist gave me an example of an exercise they used to conduct at his camp, about gender relations, with a similar message to Per-C. They'd set up folding chairs in two group-ings facing each other across an empty room. They'd have the boys and girls divide themselves between the two sets of chairs. First, they'd ask the boys a series of questions, telling them to stand if their answer was yes, each question getting more per-sonal than the last. They'd start with, "Do you like sports," and end with, "Have you been shot at or stabbed?" This would provide a chance for the girls to witness the boys' confessions. After the boys were finished answering, they'd get a chance to play witness to the girls when the staff would repeat the same process using a different set of questions. This time, they ranged from, "Do you read fashion magazines," to, "Have you been raped or sexually assaulted?" The idea behind such an uncomfortable querying was twofold, one to show power in numbers, to allow campers the safety in which to confront their fears about gender freely, to be unburdened of the pres-sure of gender, and to find solidarity in the struggles of having to deal with gender in other less safe environments. Secondly, it was to give an audience to the other, for educational purpos-es, to see how stark some of the numbers are up close when it comes to gender-influenced shaming and violence, so that boys could see how their attitudes and actions affect girls, and the girls could see how their attitudes and actions affect boys. After it was over with, they'd have a comprehensive processing session where all the campers were given the opportunity to ask questions of the now not-so-opposite sex. The activist said:

> The gender program was a miracle worker, we'd done it
> for ten straight years with stunning results, these kids would
> really respect each other after it was over with, and not in

that fake way where they learn to use the right language and continue to participate in the same behaviors of abusers and abused. They'd truly see each other as equals afterwards. You could tell by their open body language.

Except for one year, when based on our success over the years with a few at-risk youths, we'd been asked by a family court judge to put on an exclusive camp for foster care children. We didn't think to alter our gender program accordingly. When we got to questions about violence and rape, these kids went crazy, throwing their chairs around the room, getting into fights, crying and yelling. We almost had a real riot on our hands. We did have mental health counselors on staff like we always did, in case anything illegal was unveiled, but there just weren't enough counselors to cover everyone who was there who had dealt with a severe trauma in their lives, and sadly, we hadn't been accounting for how poverty played a role in that, and how traditionally pricing our camp at modest but still mostly unaffordable rate for these grant receiving kids meant that we had been limiting who had access to our camp, and therefore, fudging our numbers.

We failed to see how such traumas could normally be overcome in the midst of a few hurt kids surrounded by more well-off ones with the capacity to care for them, born out of a life not deprived of resources and love. But these kids had all been victimized in some way (by all of us) and had lost whatever trust in others (in a completely understandable way) that was needed to receive that care, so we did more harm than good, opening wounds without providing the time or fresh air (or money) to heal those wounds. I kind of feel like Per-C made the same mistake. What he was saying with his mural was good, but he failed to consider his audience, to consider what burdens they might be bearing.[18]

---

18   Anonymous, Personal Interview, April 15, 2017.

It seemed to me that these inherently varied and contradictory responses to events make up the raw material of any story (and of the critical reception to stories). The world comes to us as filtered, and what the filter allows in or removes is a little different for everyone (sometimes it's a lot different).[19] Yet, I still think the space for the possibility of a universal interpretation to Per-C and 'Dusa should be preserved,[20] so that we might all learn from it. Here, I'd like to draw attention to how the three reactions covered so far seem to maintain an inherently similar shape even in the variance of the responses. Consider again how the freedom from shame—like in the attorney's response—is not always positive. Shame can color our behavior in good ways, conditioning socially acceptable reflections in instances of moral decision making. Removing that shame could lead to one violating another[21]—as in the second response from the woman who felt Per-C violated her[22]—and that such responses as freedom from shame and shame at violation are both culturally conditioned by programs of gender, inherently shaped by the fundamental traumas of our communities, which are also intersected (and even created by) our membership in an economic class, which is just as, if not more, shameful than gender—like in our third example by the social activist. Because of this connection of movement into and through shame, we might say that Per-C's event evoked a continuum between the desire for beauty and the frustration of realizing its unattainability, its transitory nature,

---

19   And sometimes different means painful.

20   For an excellent article on how we seek the universal whether or not it exists, please see:

Knausgaard, Gunther. "The Word of God: The Cognitive Authority in a Search for Universal Truth." *Journal of Nordic Studies*, 38(2), 2007, pp. 254-275.

21   I'd like to stress that I'm not judging the attorney here. I'm not saying her shame being removed provoked immoral action in her, merely rereading the idea of shame that comes from her story to draw connections to a pattern in the idea of shame in general.

22   It also might be useful to think about how anonymity in the graffiti artist is symbolic of a sort of pure shamelessness, because there is no voice to shame, only a name on a wall.

which again seems a struggle between the universal beauty and the particular loss of its possibility for truth, which becomes a truth in and of itself and deflects from the material reality that conditions us to see one thing as beautiful and another as not.

Here we should look to the idea of geometric shape,[23] particularly the idea of a shape that can comprise the diverse particular within the intersected universal. I speak, of course, of the fractal, that combines fragments of self-similarity (or more accurately, affinity), into a whole self-similar (or affine) shape, so that by looking closer, by drawing connections to what is similar in what we initially perceive as a chaotic difference, we reveal a universal structure of infinite complexity. Could the many varied interconnected reactions to Per-C's artwork reveal a fractal shape? H.R. Parks, the famous phenomenological narrative theorist, posits that all stories have a fractal shape:

> Story logic is a phenomenological logic, and, more importantly, a fractal logic, simultaneously inductive and deductive, general and particular, multi-directional flows of information inherently dependent on each other for an expansion that contracts in on itself *ad infinitum*, moving both inward and outward according to the iterations of rules, like a cultural breathing from interior to exterior and back again; additionally, like fractal shapes, in narratives, we can trace symmetries under magnification across various scales and find patterns of similarity between each tale, the genre it belongs to, the tradition which formed that genre, and the perception of humanity which forms the tradition.[24]

---

23   We should note that shape as a geometrical concept and how it applies symmetry is inherently linked to logic within our cognitive perceptual systems, like stories are. This idea will become more important shortly. For more on perception as a form of geometry, please see:

Min, Chuck. *Visual Symmetry: The Synonymous Nature of Truth and Beauty.* Cambridge, UK: Oxford UP, 1998.

24   Parks, H.R. "Fractal Narrative: The Chaos of Beginning, Middle, and End." *Narratology Today*, 33(4), Ohio UP, 2005, p. 352.

When we consider again the idea of the interconnection between geometry and logic, it is important to note that Parks here isn't just saying that stories work according to a verbal fractal logic, rather Parks says all logic creates real interior space, like our outer space, and both spaces are inherently fractalized because we must perceive them, creating worlds inside of worlds inside of worlds.[25] His most clear example of such a phenomenon is how video game programmers have advanced the realism of the visual worlds of video games exponentially since their first beginnings of programming fractal logic to create the backgrounds to our favorite button-pushing quests.[26]

Condensing memory to expand reality through a movement from general to particular and back out to general again fundamentally embodies how I came to understand the Per-C story, and how I came to craft it.[27] As such, I will say that this story became an obsession of mine not because of what I learned about Per-C from my subjects, but because of what I learned about myself by searching for Per-C's truth, which was also a search for meaning at the grandest scales of human understanding, where gods and universes do battle with each other, and most certainly how it grounded me inside the

---

25   He might say that by just talking about Per-C, by attempting to organize our thoughts, we recreate an iteration of the real event, a double inside the interior of imagination, which must take certain real aspects of the event to be successful at drawing from it.

26   This process works so well because fractal logic can use less memory, only needing to account for a few rough structures that produce so many of the same forms (e.g., how coastlines, tree branches, and the capillary networks of lungs have roughly the same shapes). Therefore, the game can use more memory on story content and less on scenery, the picture needs only a few iterative functions to draw itself.

27   Note how I had to look at what was the same and what was different and figure out a shape that could account for all of it. I had to make a fractal of my own, which certainly must be contained within the fractal social narrative that made Per-C a story to begin with. Additionally, to even begin to understand it, I also had to modify my own understanding so that my perception could link up with the social narrative. Thus, I am also shaped according to how I perceive what happened to Per-C and 'Dusa.

material conditions I find myself in today through rhetorical figures that forced me to compare and contrast. But it is still too early to draw metaphorical conclusions. First, I need to tell the story of how I came to learn of the Per-C story and how my understanding of myself as its author[28] literally relates to the Per-C event at the First City Tower, how it became fundamentally real to me, and thus, a ground on which to investigate the ongoing realness that formulates life itself.

I first became aware of the Per-C story during my doctoral candidacy, after signing up to audit "SOCI 4378, The Politics of Pimpin'," which was taught by the famous Houston rap-

---

28 Before anyone accuses me of using a tired meta-narrative structure, with an even tireder academically faux-authoritative narrator, I should offer you my purposes here. One, narrative is inherently self-referential, especially Western classical narratives, and, as this relates to an essentially classical hero tale, it accuses its creator in a productive way, asking the reader to be critical of the assertions behind one's agency and to ask what it is we even mean by a word like universal (or a word like classical, for that matter). Therefore, I do not want to try and hide from you my long career of study at Western academic institutions and the formal methods for dictating thought that have been ingrained into my own psyche. Yes, this story is not completely about me, but this story is also fundamentally about me and how I understand the relationship between art and being. Therefore, I'd like to place the reader within all the traditions I am drawing from so that they may see the event I'm describing as close as possible to the fractal shape as it exists inside my own head. Second, I do indeed want this analysis to feel authoritative, in that I believe intuitively that my conclusion is valid, but I also respect your right as a reader to find my authority lacking. Still, the question I'm asking is, what does it mean when real effects are produced by fantasies, and what role does authority grant to this fundamental production? Therefore, this very attempt at authority should problematize notions of the distinction between narrative, history, and argument. After-all, do not all narratives use history to produce an argument within the reader? Additionally, do scholars like me merely participate in a grand semantical hijacking of language, an attempt to have it serve a pedagogical hegemony which favors larger Western capitalist patriarchal and racial hegemonies? Do we serve or defy our gods and masters when we criticize them? I would say like any confounding set of questions, we should be able to find particular cases which answer all of them as both yeses and noes on a number line of contextual continuity, and this is why I need to both show the structures of my thought behind the oral narrative I'm attempting to transcribe and the formal characteristics of my understanding of the narrative form itself. So that if you must doubt, you may come not to doubt my truth, but only my interpretation of the fundamental truth of all existence. Therefore, these overly-digressive notes should provide a rather keen insight into the way I process reality and truth, revealing the only way for me to tell this story, whether or not someone else could tell it differently.

per Professor Threat.[29] The course focused on the idea that a sort of "reverse cultural appropriation"[30] could be used as a farcical measure to both call out the larger culture's domination and to assert power in the face of that domination. Professor Threat, who was never actually a pimp but played a convincing portrait of the character of pimp on his records, spoke of the role of pimp as being the most hyperbolized example of a venture capitalist, giving real meaning to the symbolic act of exchanging capital for bodies, for stealing time and creating a market out of it, for commodifying the very recesses of a person's soul, for controlling the pleasure of the pleasureless.[31] At the time, I had been working on a project about how farce is one of the most effective methods of subversion of a dominant culture, and so Threat's description of the pimp as a capitalist farce in the course catalogue had appealed to me, and because the ability to audit classes for free was one of the few valuable perks we were given as doctoral candidates, I decided to take advantage of it.

---

29   In the early '90s, at the height of gangster rap, Threat was an emcee in the local super group known simply as Real Shit. They were essentially the Third Coast's answer to the Wu-Tang Clan, as Threat himself told me. He doesn't like this observation, but I'd also classify them as a bit of a perverted and violent Village People, each emcee embodying a different type of criminality. Professor Threat was the Pimp, Fat Chin the Mobster, Eddie P the bookie, Jeezus the crooked preacher, and Lawyer Joe, well, the lawyer. Like the Village People used popularized American archetypes to open up spaces for queerness to exist within those archetypes, Real Shit used the likenesses of less-revered stereotypes to show the fundamental lack of space that existed to allow enough black men to assume respectable roles in the public space. It as if they were saying we'll exist as infinitely more threatening than your worst nightmares unless you find room for us, which certainly comes across in such controversial tracks as "Reverse Lynchin'," "Cop Killing Blues," and "Tradin' White Hoez for White Blow."

30   Threat uses this idea of a "reverse" to lampoon the frequently held notion by whites of reverse racism, a charge Real Shit was accused of quite publicly, because of their frequent uses of the word "cracker." But Threat would note that the term "cracker" actually comes from slave masters cracking whips across black men's backs and so is still formed by white racism. Threat probably also wouldn't truly believe what he was doing was a cultural appropriation, only that it mimicked its form to critique white supremacy as a form of anti-culture.

31   Note here, how in a capitalist society, according to Threat's definition, the roles of pimp, musician, artist, and author seem to contain some rather broad areas of overlap.

However, examining farce in Threat's class threatened to undo my whole dissertation. What I found in the pimp figure as farce was a certain impotence, that while he did draw attention to the problematic of capital as virtue, the pimp on the whole didn't draw enough attention from the larger culture, even with the flashy suits and jewelry, to have any sort of real impact in undoing that same system. The pimp was powerless to resist the role that interpolated him,[32] and this role might have been a role white America needed him to play, so that they could still keep a claim on their faux morality. Additionally, the pimp actually reinforced quite a few destructive and immoral norms in a patriarchal culture's ingrained responses to women. Furthermore, my initial reactions to Threat as a person, to those times he would smile with those gold teeth after saying something awful about women left me disgusted.

However, because of how unconscious racial narratives might have been running through my own head, the problems I had with his gender narratives made me that much more uncomfortable because of my own violent response to his ideas. After all, while I loathed the venture capitalists he attempted to lampoon, I wouldn't say my reaction to them had the same visceral vitriol as my initial reactions to Threat did. Also, with a name like Professor Threat, didn't he want me to react in such a way, to prove his central thesis about how white culture (or its lack of culture) responded to black men, especially to those black men with the audacity to celebrate the achievement of wealth through traditionally unethical means by playing the parts of cartoon CEOs? Threat once said in class:

> Shit, in a patriarchy, if you want to go after they men, you go after they women. If the pimp ain't controlling them,

---

32 Which we could say also made him a prostitute—by which I mean the cultural idea of the prostitute as property and not the actual sex workers who may or may not have been victims depending on each individual arrangement—and breaks down the distinction between the seller and the sold.

the CEO is, believe that. That's why white bitches is especially valuable. Simple as Simon. You see, that's what the pimp figured out. Life ain't about playing by the rules, it's about twisting they rules so everybody else can see they malleable as a motherfucker. But look, it's a selling pussy game, right? They gonna be bitches sellin' pussy whether or not any pimp out there runnin' his hustle.

On an intellectual level, it made sense what he was saying, selling sex wasn't exclusive to pimps, and selling white sex made more money simply because of existing power dynamics making white everything more valuable, and none of it would go away because some of us didn't like it. Still, the idea of gaining equity for black men through the domination of white women left me deeply offended and deeply afraid, and this feeling of fear ultimately made me feel guilty. It was especially difficult after I raised my hand and asked if he could stop calling women bitches in class. He responded by saying, "Look, I don't mean no offense, it's just the game is the game and those who play the game get called what the game call them, and for some, the game call them bitches."

When he said it, I stormed out of class for forever—or at least, that was what it felt like at the time. Shortly after it happened, I ran into Threat at a faculty mixer, meant to promote interdisciplinary discussion among colleagues of fields that don't normally intermingle. Threat pulled me aside to apologize:

I'm sorry that I called you out in front of the class. The thing is the university pays me to be the Professor Threat character, you know? Like they want authenticity and shit, a real diverse perspective for white people, unfiltered. But like I created that character when I was twenty-five, in the 1990s, life was so different then. I ain't really about all that pussy and bitches shit anymore, it's just some shit I've been saying for so long, there's pressure for me to keep saying it, from all sides. But like I didn't want to offend you either. Can I take you out to lunch sometime to make up for it?

I said yes, not knowing it would lead to such an engaging and lasting relationship. It wasn't even meant to be a date, I don't think, but that's what ended up happening. I don't know quite how to explain it, but like when we got together just the two of us, it was as if Threat became a wholly different person, especially since he asked me to just call him Greg. At lunch, we continued to talk about the roles we played, and I found myself less and less afraid and more and more open to getting to know him better. I kept wondering if there were a way to transfer this personal overcoming of cognitive dissonance into a lasting solidarity that could transcend barriers for all people. I still wonder that now, as I'm happy to report that Greg and I recently celebrated our five-year anniversary together, even as our larger culture still seems mostly divided along racial and gender lines, divisions that keep us locked in step with those venture capitalists who sell us mini-revolutions to keep the real one from happening. In any case, we should also note that Greg's and I's relationship to class (and to each other through class) was interesting, to say the least, as he grew up working class until becoming a rich semi-famous rapper who owned a record label, and I came from a petit bourgeois family that owned a small chain of restaurants, even though at the time I met Greg, I was surviving off the pittance of a doctoral candidate's stipend, having given up my part of the family inheritance.

During lunch that day, Greg asked a set of questions so profound I couldn't shake them:

You ever feel like you're just a character in some white man's story? That the reason we can't get over oppression is because we're engulfed in the conflicts he creates for us? That we separate sex and race into categories to provoke the conflict necessary to make up any plot, and that plots are inherently monopoly capitalistic? Like, is the arche-type of the CEO the author of all our stories, consigning us to serve his will so that we might eat?

It was questions like this that made me come to fall in love with him, the way he could break apart the world and make you see it in this totally new way. When he asked me about if I was just a man's idea of a woman,[33] it struck me that my entire life, my problem with finding a feminism that fit me, with finding a theory to conform to what I really felt as a woman, was how the category of woman had probably first been assigned by a man, this classical paradox which couldn't be escaped, that man invented woman to produce a hierarchy he found himself on top of. Therefore, to assert myself as a woman was to assert myself as what man wanted to leave as a lack in himself, and I didn't want any part of that anymore than I wanted to be a second-class citizen. It also struck me how this was what made it impossible to be a man, that this search for a partner to share life with wasn't ever a search for an equal teammate but a search for what those before him had already described as undesirable, made even worse by the fact that the search for a partner was supposed be a search for some ideal happiness not based in reality, and as such, a happiness that no real woman could actually provide, since it didn't exist outside of subjective thought. Man was always destined to be disappointed, which might have been why he also wanted a woman to take his frus-trations out on. This perpetual cycle always prevents us from bridging our gaps, no matter how much moving we try to do.[34]

Yet, dating Greg made me rethink the ideas about gender that were provoked by his questions. Because our relationship

_____

33   Of course, I had read enough theory by that point that it wasn't the first time I'd consid-ered such questions, but the way he asked the question was unique and gave me a new way in which to consider the idea, a way that proved fruitful to understanding what Per-C was doing.

34   This very cycle is I think what Per-C was trying to illustrate, the freedom of femininity as represented by any anonymous man.

really felt like it took place on equal footing. After we moved in together, he'd cook three days a week, I'd cook the other three, and we'd go out once every Saturday to treat ourselves. We'd also take turns with the dishes and taking out the garbage, and not that I want to get to into the details, but our sex life was quite rewarding, he took care of me, so to speak, and he never pressured me to do anything I didn't want to do.[35]

The things I struggled with in our relationship had less to do with gender and more to do with race. Like I wasn't sure if I was so attracted to him because I hadn't expected him to turn out to be as smart as he was (and I didn't know what the lowering of my initial expectations might have said about me) or because I was technically sort of his student when we met (I started attending his class again after we had lunch, although not as regularly)[36] or if I had just bought into the cultural exoticizing of black men that white people so often participated in, which made some sense considering how capitalism values

---

35   You may be wondering, aside from the obvious relation to gender problems, what Greg's and I's relationship has anything to do with the rest of this story. I can assure you that I'll be moving back to the main thread again shortly, and that when I do, this connection will begin to become more apparent.

36   The character he played in class still irked me. Like I didn't entirely know how to take it when someone I was dating would say something like, "Wherever there's pussy to slang, there gonna be a pimp tryin' to get in on some of that. Plus, the best hoes, they like the pimp, there a certain freedom that comes when someone is managing yo time and money for you. I know it sounds shitty, but some people seek that kind of shit out, like in those restrictions, they can be who they want to be without worrying. They can feel safe, and so the best pimp, he got to keep his hoes safe, gotta respect 'em. It's more nuanced than the violent bullshit they put in the movies, even if it's also fundamentally more violent than we imagine it to be." Again, what he was saying might have been true, and sure some of it was empty posturing on his part, but there seemed like better ways to express it to me, and I had hoped to push him in new directions, although I must admit I probably didn't (and still don't) push him as much as I maybe should about what he says in public—if I even have a right to push him. But like when we're alone together, he doesn't talk like that, not really, and usually, as cliché as it sounds, he really does complete me, and I'm not sure I could do the same for someone else with my own racially provoked responses if the roles were reversed, so it's all this giant ball of confusion anyway. That's before we even get into the idea of how he eventually paid my student loans off for me when we got married after I had refused my father on that same offer so many years before, and how that made me into something like a prodigal class traitor.

otherness as a commodity, and how it teaches us to desire commodities. Still, I don't think I was using Greg, the fact that I cared about him so deeply led me to feel secure in that fact, and I still don't entirely know the answers to any of the identity questions our relationship raised and still raises, but I do know that Greg helped me realize how the theories I so learned to traffic in as a cultural critic often proved incapable of explaining the messiness of how real human relationships are formed, and how those interactions occur in contradictory motions on all levels, making the question of desire infinitely more complex[37] than chalking it up to a phenomenon capitalism could fully explain, even if the quest for capital definitely causes us to traffic in desires' excesses, and even if that process certainly comes to bear on our romances, still we can hardly ever even begin to fully parse desire when we actually try to write about the experience of its influence on both the accumulation of resources and the connections we have with other people. We only ever get as far as explaining that we have desires for things we don't like to desire and for things we don't need, that our desires for freedom and autonomy often impinge on others' desires for freedom and autonomy, and that desire doesn't always necessarily influence how we love each other, but we fail to show the inherent elusive quality that imagination creates in desire, and how that natural process retroactively affects our theories of identity formation and of social change, certainly no different on the individual level of Greg's and I's desires for each other and the social arrangement that molded us into a couple as a result of this dynamic. I guess to put it more simply, sometimes not knowing how the gravy gets made helps you enjoy the gravy more.

But what I can say for sure is that Greg and I really fell in love

---

37 Think again of the fractal, how our relationships exist not just in one to one interactions but also in one person's own psyche in the ideal relationship they have with themselves, which is formed in conversation with all the relationships they've ever observed, both real and fictional, which are all conversations with all the relationships those people have ever observed. Thus, breaking any of this kind of stuff apart and applying a unifying thread will never exactly work, but it also won't ever exactly fail either.

during our discussions over Per-C, and that this might have been in part because of a self-similarity in our understanding of ourselves in terms of Per-C and 'Dusa as characters, how we also played the roles of hero and furious goddess. In fact, I heard about Per-C for the first time in Greg's class. He was discussing the intersection between the pimp figure and other figures in hip-hop culture, showing how the pimp inspired those figures. He played a track from G-Spot Jonez[38] called "Hoe Magic." The hook had the lines: "Cut yo head off, / Tag it in the sky / like Per-C flipped 'Dusa / made all dem bitches cry." Greg talked about how Per-C had gotten his start painting gorgon heads all over the city of Houston, at locations increasingly more traveled. He started on gas station walls, trapping a few random men in the gaze, and eventually, he was painting the sides of the courthouse, keeping the city business from operating on schedule.[39] I had studied Medusa way back during my undergraduate career, in the early days of my introduction to the theoretical, when I had caught a particular bug

---

38   This was my first time hearing Jonez, or much of any rap music for that matter. I had an intellectual understanding of what rap was supposed to do, but I'd never sat down and explored the form. Maybe it was the fact that Greg's vulgarity had begun to rub off on me, that I had come to treat vulgarity as more harmless than I did previously, but it was like hearing rap music for the first time again that day. Greg turned me on to a whole lot of other Houston rappers who referenced Per-C in their songs, and I must say that on some level, my obsession by the Per-C story was fueled by a budding obsession with rap music as a form. For an introductory playlist, see:

1. Real Shit. "Decapitate and Penetrate (Ya Mind)." Rap-A-Lot Records, 2002.
2. Steve tha Sleeze. "Tag, You Ain't It." Dopehouse, 2004.
3. Tha Copz. "Buff That Shit." 187 LPs, 2009.
4. Take This Mafia. "What Ya Looking At, Fool?" Atlantic Records, 2008.
5. Stillborn. "Stonefaced Killa." Rap-A-Lot Records, 2011.
6. Jihad. "Explosions in tha Sky." Safe Boy Records, 2013.
7. Jeezus. "Hero Game." Rap-A-Lot Records, 2004.
8. Big Lazy. "I Can't Move." Dopehouse, 2003.
9. Whitey Rhymes."Appropriate This." Capital Records, 2009.
10. Lil' Big. "Shame." 187 LPs, 2010.

39   The slow waiting time for service was something the Houston courthouse really didn't need any extra help with. Probably one of the myriad reasons the Mayor hated him so much.

for French feminist anthropological psychoanalysts.[40] When the names of Per-C and 'Dusa jumped out at me, I raised my hand and asked, "If Per-C was such a disruptive figure in the city, how come I've never heard of him before? I grew up here, seems like I would have heard something."

Greg smiled at me, the glint of his grill lighting up the whole classroom, bright with the possibility of a new study.[41] He said, "Shit, a city is the perfect place to forget about culture. Sometimes stories are just like that, they just don't reach your ear, but when they do, shit, it'll change your whole world. You wanna know about Per-C? Start asking around. Might surprise you."

I didn't ask around, not at first. Instead, I did what I always did when stories intrigued me. I searched the article databases on the Rice library website. It didn't matter how many cross-references I ran, how many search terms I used, how many keywords I tried to think of relating to street art, contemporary art, classical repurposing, appropriation, the role of the hero, and so on, I turned back one single result, not even from a doctor, only a Master's thesis from someone named Mike Hilbig, who I also could find nothing else about after I later searched for other articles by him. There was no

---

40   To give you an idea of what I was reading, the texts I used to cite most in class, texts I probably didn't truly even understand, having read none of the psychoanalytical foundational materials yet, but those articles were probably as follows:

Dubois, Simone. "Medusa: The Classical Idea of Artificial Intelligence in the Female Perspective." Trans. by Amy Flanders, *The Poststructuralist* 45(8), 1987, pp. 567-89.

Thomas, Renée. *Helen: The Perverse Woman in Ancient Greece.* Trans. by Nell O'Connor, Cambridge, UK: Oxford UP, 1991.

Morel, Sophie. "The Castrated Man: Transcending the Identity of Patriarchy by Rereading the Fragments of Forefathers." Trans. by Dorothy Flowers, *Journal of the Second Wave* 11(7), 1975, pp. 230-238.   Also, see Note 3.

41   Note that my reaction to his smile here was also an antithesis in interpretation to my initial reaction to his smile.

sight of him on social media or People Finder either. Either Hilbig was an alias, or the guy was a hermit who'd never published a single thing after leaving grad school.

His thesis wasn't any more enlightening about Per-C than my search terms. Essentially, he wrote a bloated treatise on the classical story of Perseus with a few references to the masterpiece Per-C painted, references I'd already gotten from Greg. Also, Hilbig's suggestion for knowing Per-C was the same as Greg's: ask around. His final conclusion was that the story was too complex to portray the full meaning of in one stream of words,[42] so that to understand Per-C's "psychoanalytic Tower of Babel," as Hilbig called it, one had to confront the difficulty of seeing all the different people whose lives it affected struggle to say just what it was that made it such a life-changing artwork. Then, Hilbig talked about some seemingly unconnected ideas about simulation theory, about how our lives might have been programmed by a computer, that the mathematical probability of such a scenario was actually quite high considering all we'd already simulated on a computer, how if we had figured out how to simulate ourselves completely at any point in the future, we'd likely be simulations of ourselves now. He said this would explain Per-C, but he didn't say how.

I couldn't make any sense of it. Was he trying to say that Per-C simulated another world? Was he trying to suggest that none of it matters because we're probably just artificial intelligences, results of random programming[43] put in by some higher level force, that DNA controls so much more than we give it credit for? Was he saying that our thoughts seem to

---

42   I guess I'd agree with him, which is why I'm writing more about my reaction to finding the story than the story itself, after having failed numerous times to write this very article, never thinking I got the story completely "right."

43   At the time, I hadn't yet stumbled upon Parks' Fractal Theory, if I had, it might have made a bit more sense. I think Hilbig was alluding to how worlds open up from stories, and what the implications of such a stance might be, but we're not yet to the implications portion of our narrative argument, so I'll hold on to my interpretation for a bit longer.

form from a will of their own? There were certainly conclusions that could have been drawn, but there simply wasn't enough context yet for me to draw from. Worse yet, when I went back to reread Hilbig's thesis, I couldn't find the document anywhere,[44] like someone had erased it from the article database or I had made it up in some sort of a strange dream.

I took Greg's and Hilbig's advice. I started asking around. I was surprised. Once I'd been alerted to the notion of Per-C's existence, of his real history, mentions of Per-C started popping up everywhere (even if there were still no information in the article databases).[45] When I went to see a Cy Twombly exhibit at the Menil, they were selling 'Dusa tote bags. When I went to Papasito's for dinner, they had a drink called a Dancing 'Rita with a little 'Dusa head on the glass. And when I started listening to 97.9, The Box, for research purposes, I kept hearing Per-C's name popping up over and over again on so many different tracks.

I began asking people about Per-C everywhere I went. It was like everyone I talked to had been there or knew someone who was there or knew someone who knew someone who was there. I started recording their responses on an app on my smartphone, staying up late at night transcribing them, trying to fill in the gaps. The interpretations of everyone involved were so strange and disparate, and, as a scholar, it's always harder, a little more fraudulent feeling, when the evidence you're working with is almost one hundred percent anecdotal. I eventually developed a questionnaire that I'd have people

---

44   The reason I haven't cited it here.

45   When I asked Greg why he thought Per-C might be so prominent in the regular culture but was still studied by no one, he had two theories: 1) it was a local story and simply didn't generate enough national interest for scholars, and 2) Per-C painted right around the turn of the millennium when, true, we already had internet, but we didn't really have The Internet yet, that Per-C probably never found a proper cyber home and was thus forgotten about. On that second theory, this is perhaps tangential, but once again Greg opened up a world for me, making me think how The Internet might actually be a machine made for forgetting, how it formally privileges keeping only certain kinds of information, that knowledge will never allow itself to be constrained to one human form.

fill out, which made cataloging the data a bit easier, but I also failed to provide a structure that would further illuminate the thing I was searching for.[46] One woman wrote:

> Hard to say how I felt. Like sure it was against my will to be painted like that, it made me uncomfortable, but what could I do about it after it was over with? It happened. There were more important things to worry about than what it meant, than if I should do something about it. I had kids to feed.[47]

The implanted memory theory also came up again:

> I think its like that Mandela Effect thing. You ever hear of that? How Mandela died in prison in the '80s but we forgot he did, so then he died again in 2013, after we'd crossed into some alternate version of reality. Say it happened with the *Berenstain Bears* too, that people say it was spelled *Berenstein*, with an 'e,' wherever it is we originally come from. Then there's how Queen's *We Are the Champions* doesn't say 'of the world' at the end of the last chorus like everyone seems to remember. That was the one that most fucked me up. But really, for my money, I think the Per-C thing never happened, we just started talking about it like it did, because some rappers were fucking with us, playing a prank on us, or just testing out some elaborate performance art, writing a new mythology, and then it snowballed into a real history, and now we have real memories of that shit.
>
> They spread like viruses, you know, histories do. Once you rewrite the past, the future gets all mutated. It could feel like crossing into a different dimension. But that's probably just some bullshit we dream up to help us forget how easily our memories can get bullshitted, because we don't

---

46 Which was also a bit vague.

47 Anonymous, Personal Interview, Jan 3, 2014.

want to distort the concrete perceptions of ourselves.[48]

Then, once again, there were people who were angry. A woman who I met in a laundromat told me:

> Any woman doesn't have a right to her body is what it tells me, but I'm also a little concerned here especially with the ramifications for women of color, disabled women, transgender and queer women he painted. Marginalized groups, especially those of us that exist in the intersections between one form of oppression and another, have fought hard to even have a voice with which to tell our own stories, to become artists who can represent our own struggles, and then you get these fucking white dudes[49] that come along and want to dictate what our cultures are supposed to be about, want to tell us what they see in us, what they care about in us, like they keep trying to imagine it, because they won't just do the fucking research.[50]

---

48   Anonymous, Personal Interview, August 18, 2015.
This interview in particular drew me back to Hilbig's ideas on simulation theory. Like if we were a program, what would happen if we were made to believe something that might have never happened?

49   This was another fact that would force me to confront my own racism. Because I had assumed Per-C was black when I first started my research. Greg would later confirm what this woman had told me, how most revered graffiti writers were actually white kids in an all out rejection of what middle class petty bourgeois life called them to. He told me the interesting thing was how it was almost like an appropriation of an appropriation of an appropriation of black culture responding to white culture. He talked about how this is the central problem with all politics of appropriation, that cultures always hybridize in zones of intersection, that appropriation is a natural result of the human phenomenon of learning through imitation, but that because of power differences that exist prior to ourselves within our larger American culture, when white people appropriated culture, there were often consequences that came along with holding white capitalist power structures in place, of giving whites possession of cultures they hadn't formed, possessions which could be sold back to the public in the form of exploitative commodities. I asked him what it meant that I would have to appropriate to tell the Per-C story, he said, "What it really comes down to is trying to be respectful, of knowing your material, and of keeping the knowledge of your privilege at the forefront of your discussion." I hope I am doing that within this very text and imagine I have both succeeded and failed.

50   Anonymous, Personal Interview, May 13, 2014

As I continued to collect interviews and questionnaires, and as I continued my futile search through archival data for traces of the Per-C story, all the while looking for some sort of fundamental generative principle in his work, questions kept unfolding. What does it mean to consider the audience of an artwork in an urban public space, especially one as diverse as Houston? Could one ever appeal to all cultures without provoking or being insensitive toward a certain group's culture or identity? Is there a such thing as a pure art that can find a universal recognition?

In thinking about what art was and how it could be pure, I came to think about the form of graffiti in general. While many have studied graffiti in connection with the politics of public space and land ownership, few have studied how the erasure of tags from such public spaces creates room for oral narratives to flourish about its most revered practitioners. I would argue that the erasure (in conjunction with the artist's anonymity) shows the inherently private goals of a defilement of the public. Additionally, through erasure, graffiti is meant to be seen and not seen. In connection to Per-C, I'd like to note here how his tradition of graffiti might have shown that he had little concern for audience, that who he hurt didn't fundamentally matter to the questions he provoked, as morally correct or incorrect as you might interpret such a position. Of course, graffiti is inherently connected to language, some even going as far as to call the form a "pure ekphrasis,"[51] which

---

51   This notion should probably first be credited to GIRTH, a writer out of Portland, Oregon who published a short zine called "Bomb it to Shredz!," where he called graffiti "reverse writing," the way it uses paint to put language in your head, instead of using language to paint a picture. However, Mr. GIRTH does not seem aware of this closeness in definition to that of the western classical idea of ekphrasis, the verbal representation of the visual, and vice versa, nor is his independently published zine easy to find. Thus, for the best academic treatise—which is, admittedly, an outsider perspective on "outsider art" but still treats the subject with a proper respect, please see:

Dylan, Peter. "Verbal Representation in the Aesthetics of Vandalism: The Graffitist," *Journal of Outsider Arts*, 25(2), U of Colorado P, 2010.

is a sort of unified chaos, in that neither the graphic nor the lingual form can take precedence for ordering, and as ordering requires hierarchy and is also required for understanding, ekphrasis always leaves details out, details that complicate the very idea of what a word can do, especially as it comes to the process of identification. Graffiti starts with this simple idea of a word stylized on a wall,[52] assumed as a name for an artist, a form of identity. However, this identifying mark is also destined for erasure, painted in the knowledge of how public works departments and police officers will buff a work off of a wall to maintain the drabness of a concrete urban environment. In fact, the famous French psycholinguist Marlena Petit says all identifying marks are forms of erasure:

> Each identifying mark tells a whole life story, embodies a whole history,[53] revealing a culture of the self all of its own, and yet, each mark left is a permission to forget, a memory not worth saving, in other words, an identifying mark is a vision of how a whole history is always an incomplete retelling.[54]

If all attempts at preserving culture, at writing history, are forms of erasure that seek permanence, how does the purpose of a graffiti writer differ from the classical purpose of art as a way of maintaining this permanence?

Here, I will argue that graffiti artists do, in fact, seek permanence like other artists whose words and pictures are

---

52   We should also note how graffiti isn't so different a practice from what ancient man painted and etched on temples and monuments throughout antiquity, how the illegality of graffiti is a thoroughly modern idea, one that comes from an attempt to control who writes history, which has privileged the book form in the power class since the dawning of the printing press.

53   Note, here, again, another idea that seems to maintain a symmetry across scale like a fractal.

54   Petit, Marlena. *Identity and History: The Self as a Writing Culture.* New York: NYU Press, 2001, p. 123.

longer lasting, but this permanence is not in the work itself. The permanence comes from how it causes us to forget the self, by wrapping it in a shroud of mystery, a shroud which when removed unveils the nothingness of our quests. Therefore, in graffiti, where men *qua nom de plumes*, wholly anonymous men, leave a presence in the absence of an artist to take credit for the work, this presence destined for absence charges itself as a preprogrammed energy of memory, which releases itself in the form of a story.

In the end, that was the most I could come up with about why Per-C was important, because structurally he had to be important, because personally, he had been the spark that caused an especially important relationship to form between Greg and I, but there was one other conclusion I kept coming back to, purely speculative, but intuitively I feel I should share it. Because I kept thinking, what if fractals aren't perception? What if fractals are how the real is actually organized? What if we're a literal program, not in the DNA sense, but like an actual simulated program, like the Hilbig thesis suggested, how we might be all living in a universe not of our own design, a universe in which implanting memories would be easy to do, would just take the click of a mouse in some larger universe we're contained inside? I kept thinking back to that mysterious Master's student, like how his thesis had provided me with this untranslatable cypher that still ended up formulating and structuring so much of how I approached the Per-C story. I kept thinking back to how I used to read books as a kid, how I always felt like there was some code to be cracked that could allow me to see behind the veil, that would take me to some literal alternate realm where I might see the truth behind this strange thing we call consciousness. I started reading like that again sometime while I was searching for Per-C, and I must admit I still wait some days for the oxygen to separate like a pair of curtains from in front of my face, for God to be standing there on an infinitely large stage, telling me why I was created, telling me what I was supposed to be, how I was supposed to be, what role was the "right" role for me, and how I could escape the misreadings of my peers in the face of that role.

So here's where I take the leap, when Greg asked me if we were "characters in some white man's story," maybe that metaphorical question was an actual truth. Maybe Mike Hilbig is our god, maybe he left little clues behind in all the books and articles we read, which are all fundamentally a part of his voice, of his desire, of his creation, what if he's not even that noble or omnipotent or all-loving, what if we're just a product to sell someone, characters in a story that's only value is in helping keep Hilbig's dream alive of being able to quit his real job to be a full-time creator one day, or what if he just appropriates us as characters to try to figure out what's wrong with himself, the way I recreated the Per-C narrative to struggle with what it means to be a woman in a man's world? I wonder who all might read this, and in what dimensions it might get read in, and I keep thinking how I offer myself for display based on this thing I can't control, and that when it all comes down to it, my whole life, my search has really been about this question that will never be satisfied by any answer, this question that I want to ask everyone else, that I want to scream at them, that I want to repeat until they get it, "What are you looking at? What are you looking at? What are you looking at?"

The Ballgame at Xibalba

After the clock for placing final bets on the game ticked down to zero, the crowd shuffled away from the ticket window and to their seats. The Referee sounded his whistle, gathered the players at half court in a circular formation around the girth of his pale flesh. His waxed bald head reflected the underground arena lights from the aerial view. He held the ball toward the rafters, in the basement of Xibalba—oil tycoon Tex Randall's mansion in River Oaks in Houston, TX, the underground square footage cost three times as much as the rest of the oversized house because of built-in supports to stabilize the structure from shifting clay soil and aquifer, essentially, it wasn't an ideal environment for a basketball tournament, which was why Tex liked it so much.

The Referee looked first at the Rookie, then at Big Daddy, then back up at the ball, brought it down to his naked waist, bounced it off the court with both hands, picked it up, held it above his head again, turned his chin upward, took a deep breath, then paused to give the crowd a chance to frame the moment against the spotlighted onyx walls before tossing up the rock to signal the start of the first half. The Rookie leapt and touched the ball first, Big Daddy too pensive, the naked referee with the whistle standing under him was too much an image outside the scope of his normal routine, he never even left his feet. Wasn't exactly the fiercest start to the battle of wills that The Order had hoped for, especially not with all the money they had paid Big Daddy to play, and especially considering the bonus opportunity should he win MVP, which he was the pregame favorite for.

The tip went to Hermes2K, legendary point guard from the And One Mix tape, his street-ball finesse a spectacle on YouTube, prolific passer, real fans remembered him as a well-known commodity going all the way back to his All-American days in high school, when he looked like a grown man playing with children, destined for the big show. Too bad a hazing scandal involving his frat lost him a scholarship to Duke only the first month into his freshman season, he never made it back onto any college team, the pros didn't deem his talent worthy of the risk. Now, like everyone else on the court, he had a chance at a second chance. He dribbled the rock past the Thanatos Bitz half-court logo—Tex's drilling company—went to the top of the key, dropped a pass down into the paint where The Rookie had posted up on Big Daddy, kid took two dribbles as he backed the grizzled veteran toward the rim, then faked a spin to his right and went left, took the rock unguarded the rest of the way to the hole. Big Daddy cursed himself as the Rookie put two on the board, wasn't expecting that kind of strength.

The crowd oohed at the slam dunk, the kid a real life American eagle when he took flight with the egg of destiny in his hands, but then as he made his way up the court to get back on defense, the ooh morphed into ridiculing murmurs. He was still new to the circuit, couldn't have been more than sixteen or seventeen years old, everyone wondered what he was doing here with this group of has-beens. Still, The Rookie didn't look like how a star talent was supposed to look either. He was as awkward when he ran as he was graceful in the air, his undersized frame not yet matching his big feet and big hips, his long neck colluding with gravity to make his head bobble like a plastic collector's item. Not to mention the pink and green workout attire or the expression on his face, the way he lowered his eyebrows when he smiled in a trying-to-belong-by-not-looking-too-much-like-I'm-trying-to-belong kind of a way.

Maybe it was this very performative naivety that made his game so captivating, the way it confounded expectations, in the end, made him a featured player at this final game of the tournament, made him second in the odds for The Golden Dagger, for MVP, at this main event for The Order, who payed the utmost homage to the big man game. The power of the throwback, as Tex, the founder, liked to say. They saw their tournament as the embrace of a budding religious tradition formed in the restructuring of the rules of an arbitrary but classical game. Their own version an antithesis to the pro game, where the post-up had been voided of its magic by progressive analytics, corresponding to a favoring of finesse over strength—an aesthetic fundamentally opposed to their own moral framework. Strength determined authority, which determined the sacred, thus making strength the primary mode of being for a true playing of the game, the days of calculating the efficiency of methods were numbered, played out, it was time to return to a purer form of competition.

And so the players behind the players, the members of The Order, who played the truly consequential games, who belonged to a timeless class of men with the literal job of building an omnipotent and homogeneous culture based entirely on power, the world depended on their success to frame power as understandable for the masses, how they saw it anyway. Their newest task to take the faux-divination of modern day fanatics and turn it into a moral and spiritual framework that could hold the proper level of real tension in a battle between two giants. Thus, they paired the two strongest street-ball big men currently playing on the national circuit, The Rookie and Big Daddy, against each other in the game inside of the game. The centers extraordinaire, the old school inspiring the new school, winner take all, provided he be prepared to make the ultimate sacrifice, to do anything to win.

The Rookie bumbled to his spot. There was something familiar about his failings, or maybe it was his face. Big Daddy shook his head, tried to get the cobwebs out, or maybe it was something in the The Rookie that had shaken his entire being, had made him remember his early years, he didn't want those mentally trying times to come back anymore than he wanted to suffer these physically trying ones. He looked away, saw his teammate Ajax, his second in command, his power forward, together, as a front court, they called themselves the Titans of the Paint, the two men both hovering around seven feet, Ajax the dirty work guy, Big Daddy the stat sheet filler. He told Ajax to take the ball out. Ajax did as he was told and tossed it in to LuLu Cypher, their point guard, who ran up the court and shot a quick mid-range jumper at the elbow just seconds into the shot clock. Bricked it off the rim. The ball kicked into the stands.

It was caught by a former president there in attendance with his wife. He looked at her and smiled as if to say, I'm proud of you even if no one else is, if for nothing more than being one of the very few women allowed into the room—the former first lady stared at The Rookie, something in his trying too hard must have produced some kernel of truth inside of her—the elder statesman smiled at her, thought she'd show them one day, she'd already shown him. He tossed the ball back in with a little extra oomph on it, heard the crowd clap behind him, he sighed, was looking forward to a vacation from all the appearances after four straight decades of campaigning, but it seemed like no matter where you went, still no way to ever shake the expectations of a crowd.

The referee caught the president's pass on the third bounce. Big Daddy gave a look of disapproval, not at the president's impotent throw, but at the betrayal of Lulu, his teammate, at the reckless offense. If they were going to win the Grand Old Prize, he'd have to do it on his own, show The Rookie why old tricks trump new talent. The referee held the ball again, stood naked for all to see, rubbed his belly like an eastern deity, the crowd all giggled, as if he had a visionary magic that went beyond just being able to call the games, that allowed him to exert actual intentional force on the dialectic between the home team and the visitors. He handed the ball off to Achilles, who had earned his name from the injury that saw him dropped from Charlotte's G-League team—the furthest he'd ever made it toward the big dance. He tossed it back in to Hermes2K who drove into the paint for a layup and was met at the rim by the firm swat of Big Daddy's gargantuan hand.

The current president pumped an approving fist toward the veteran from his court side seats. That's my guy, he said to his daughter, his date for the evening, held out his own hand, What do you think? She said, Oh yes daddy, yes, you have the biggest hands, you do, you're my Big Daddy.

When the ball bounced again at half court, Big Daddy scooped it up, dug deep, charged the length of the floor in only five fluid steps, beat everyone else and dunked it on the other end.

At the Stygian fountain, which The Order saw as the perfect symbol of movement between the multiple flows and the singular source to which they all returned, Steve Bannon stood talking to Mohammed Bin Salman. Looks like he's still got it to me, you sure you want to do this? The Saudi king nodded and offered a hand holding a wad of dollar bills, Bannon met it with another wad, took the whole thing and wrapped a rubber band around it, passed it off to Emmanuel Macron for safekeeping, the prime minister holding Bannon's hand just a little longer than was comfortable.

The Saudi chuckled and said, Sucker.

Bannon puffed out the lapels on his wrinkled suit jacket. We'll see, he said.

Then the two men, respecting the betting ritual, each took one of The Order's Golden Coins from the bowl on the platform marking the boundary for the fountain, kissed it and tossed it into the winedark waters before all three men returned to the stands. Big Daddy saw them walking from his periphery, tracked Bannon back to his seat during a time out after a foul call on Achilles. Felt the urge to punch someone. That is, until he saw a guy sitting behind Bannon wearing an alien mask—almost too realistic—maybe just a lizard mask. A lizardman? Like those Info-wars wackos (or non-wackos?) write about on the internet? Wasn't that just supposed to be antisemitic posturing? His urge for violence toward his oppressors subsided in a new kind of confusion. He felt like giving up, Big Daddy didn't know what to believe anymore, his new experiences constantly proving counter to his lived experience, eroding any sense of trust he'd ever had in any sense of rightness in the world.

It was all too much, this crazy fucking place, this crazy fucking game, he didn't know why he had agreed to it—or he knew exactly why, but he wasn't sure if his initial reasoning had been sound—shit, basketball was already a crazy enough game to begin with, how you worried about the constant risk of injury, the uncouth characters who showed up to the parks in the neighborhoods where he usually played, the constant searching for scouts among their ranks, hoping to impress on the right day, but here, in one of the richest places in Texas, surrounded by eccentric power-hungry CEOs and politicians and maybe even literal aliens, he had to ask himself if it had ever been worth it, and if he even still had it. Was he losing it, and did the pronoun refer to his mind or his destiny, and was there a difference between the two? This strange legacy of athletics he'd been called into, where the body could be acted with and acted upon at the same time, both giver and receiver, dominant and dominated, where the body was most fallible (and temporary), where no spirit could be found to carry him over to the abstract imaginary space he so needed to reach, and yet, there was simultaneously a contradictory sense that he had always been stuck inside a fantasy.

Big Daddy opened the busted screen door and came inside the tiny house that only seemed to get smaller each time he crossed the threshold. He wiped his brow with a white towel and fluffed his still damp tank top twice. Found his wife Cassandra sitting on the couch watching the television. He asked, Where are the girls?

My mom's.

He looked at the silence coming from the window unit, wished he could turn it on, but they were probably late on the bills again. He handed her a hundred dollars. She reached up without saying a word, grabbed the money and stuck it into her bra, which was visible through her own loose fitting tank top. He said, I know it's not a lot, but—

Shhh, I'm trying to watch this.

He sat down next to her on the couch, could feel a spring poking through the back, thought about all the new things they wanted and couldn't afford, most of all a college education for their two girls, they still had time to save even if the hope of having anything to save was practically nil, but he didn't want them to have to live like this when they got older, and he hoped she would approve of the plan he was about to suggest.

Cassandra's eyes had yet to shift away from the screen. A wild looking thing, not quite in the form of a man, crawled around on all fours while growling, his face covered in mud, hair matted, was locked in some kind of an observational room with gray walls. Big Daddy heard the narrator ask, But was John Doe a wolf or a man? And did the not-guilty-by-reason-of-insanity defense apply to a wolf-man? More after this.

What the fuck you watching? He asked.

National Geographic Channel. She paused, refusing to speak even through the commercials.

Okay? He invited her to keep going.

She blew out a sigh. You see, It's fucked up baby. Like this happened in America, right? These three guys go hiking up in Appalachia, they're met by this naked man on the trail who rips one of their throats out with his own teeth, the victim bleeds out quick, dead right there, it's horrific. Then, he runs back up the trail and into the forest. The other two find the police, track the naked guy's footprints and find he's living with a pack of wild dogs, doesn't seem to be cultured, like these animals might have really raised him, living in that forest in Kentucky completely unnoticed that whole time. The police wrestled him to the ground and took him in, shot all the dogs in the process. Poor guy was probably just scared of intruders. It's horrible what happened, but like he also can't communicate or anything, couldn't have known right from wrong, yet there's still some dip shit fucking Republican prosecutor who's trying to charge him with Murder One. Give him the death penalty. Turns out the kid he killed was some lily white Harvard Law student on a trip to find himself or some bullshit. But like asshole prosecutor says it doesn't matter if the guy didn't know what the law was, that an animal should be put down like an animal.

I don't believe in the death penalty, but what would you do with him? Can't lock him up in gen pop.

I wouldn't fucking kill him. Guy was raised by wolves, like in real life he was, ain't no Jungle Book story about it. We should be trying to figure out what that means about brain plasticity, or whatever they can figure out it means about whatever. We should try to teach him a language, teach him to communicate, so he can tell us something about our animal natures we might be able to understand.

But if we teach him language, don't we sort of kill the animal, death penalty or not? Once he learns how to say it, he'll lose what it is that makes him think differently, that makes him primal.

Whatever, I'm not trying to get all philosophical. Just saying it's fucked up. She pulled a rubber band off the spool that doubled as a coffee table and started to pull her hair back. Big Daddy could see her sweating, wondered if she'd let him turn on the a/c now. She continued. Like what's wrong with our country?

Hey are you hot? He asked. He pulled his arm up and rubbed the back of his neck.

Hot about not having enough fucking money, yeah. She crossed her arms and legs, scooted to the corner of the couch.

He pulled his arm down, stuffed it into his empty pocket. He said, Gave you all I got.

Yeah, yeah, I know. Look, it's Saturday, I won't get on your case today, but you know you need to get your ass a real job. This two-bit hustling shit can't cut it anymore.

About that, I got an opportunity—

Shhh, my show's coming back on.

Big Daddy tuned out, pulled out his phone and sunk into the couch. He started scrolling through his Twitter feed. Stopped on an article by NPR tweeted by Black Lives Matter Miami, his hometown activist group. The headline read, "Police Officer Hugh Davidson Confesses on National Television to Racist Killing of Jaleel Peters." He clicked on the article. Read the transcript for Davidson's press conference:

Thank you for coming today. I have spoken with my attorney, and against her advice—it was her advice that I say it was against her advice—but against her other advice, I'd like to give a statement about the Oct. 25th shooting of Jaleel Peters. I pulled over Mr. Peters at MLK and 62nd street, in front of Liberty Square, around seven p.m. that day. Upon approaching the car, I saw Mr. Peters lean over to his right. I saw his black skin and immediately thought he was grabbing for a weapon. I unholstered my gun, switched the safety into the off position and ran up to his window. I saw his registration in his hands, not a weapon like my chief reported to you last week. I squeezed the trigger despite no evidence of a gun, there was no thought behind it. Since it happened, I've been going to bed every night wondering why I so feared for my life, why I felt the need to execute this man. I can't come to any other conclusions except that I'm a bastard, and even more-so than that, a racist.

I joined the force because I once believed in the power of reform, because I heard about cases just like this of police brutality, because I heard about the abuses of power toward people of color, and truthfully, I'd heard people say things like All Cops are Bastards, but I didn't think it had to be that way. I thought I could be different, but I guess when you've been told your whole life by your family that certain neighborhoods are dangerous, and when every news station has been focused on what street gangs are at war with each other, and when the vast majority of the black characters you've seen in movies are villains, I learned a devastating lesson about what being black meant, and along with it, I adopted that same white fear waiting to be transformed into a predatory instinct. It didn't matter how much I tried to tell myself I didn't see color, how much I believed I had no prejudice in my heart. I was powerless to reform what I had already accepted as truth.

This is not to say these are excuses, I accept whatever ways this statement will hurt my case. I'm even asking that any potential jurors watching this press conference show up to court prepared to throw the book at me. I killed a man, and I need to be held accountable. Mr. Peters didn't get to choose life, and neither should I. It isn't even about justice, so much as the impossibility of it existing in this system as it's constructed.

As I've searched for some kind of answer in all of this, it's come to my attention that it was my denial of my own prejudice that made it easier for it to manifest itself in such brutality. If I had admitted to myself earlier that I was afraid of black men, I think I might have had a whole lot more chance at working through those prejudices before they became deadly, before I was consigned to a life of hating myself for what I've done. I'd ask that other police and other white people say it with me, admit to it, just try it, maybe in the mirror first, say, I am a racist. Say it before you act on it. This is who we were raised to be, and there can't be any apologies, there can't be any justice, there can't be any healing, until there's an acknowledgment of the true severity and scope of the problem. I ask you tonight to acknowledge the problem. I ask that you aspire to a morality based on something more than guilt. Then I ask that you to throw me to the wolves as a sacrifice to undo the very concept of guilt.

Big Daddy had always thought he would appreciate it the day he heard a cop just admit what most black people already knew to be true, but under the circumstances, it made him more dejected. If this cop was as liberal as he seemed to present himself, and if liberalism was the best protection black people could hope for, maybe there was no hope for black people in America. He especially felt that way when he scrolled down the page to see an update from the original post. The judge had declared Officer Davidson incompetent to stand trial. His attorney had filed an injunction to suspend all legal activity after the press conference. Said a man in his right mind would never admit to being a racist murderer on national television. Only took the judge an hour to make a ruling. Beyond a reasonable doubt, shit, seemed more like a black man needed beyond divine will to get any kind of justice in this country. Big Daddy breathed heavy, You see this?

My show.

Whatever, fuck it.

Baby, what's wrong?

This motherfucker, he said, showing her his phone. Like we can't even get a guilty verdict when a fucking pig admits to being a pig on live TV.

Oh yeah, I saw that, it's awful. You know, I suffer with you every single time you leave the house, especially when you're out there hustling for basketball winnings, thinking about how you're just a racist cop away from—

Would you please, I mean, I can fear for my life by myself. Why don't you just worry about loving me? Worry about what kind of a world we're gonna leave behind for our girls. Seems like this cop is a perfect example of the shit white people get into when they're trying to fix things.

Baby, you know it ain't like that. I just worry about you is all. I know there's certain ways we ain't never gonna see the world the same way. I'm okay with that. I feel like it makes us stronger. You got one perspective. I got another. Together, we got whatever we can put our heads to. I'm sure the girls will be fine. I love you.

I love you too. Listen, I need to talk to you. I've been trying to tell you this whole time. I've got an opportunity to put some real money in front of us, maybe even some life changing money. But I got to fly out to Houston at the end of the month—

Oh no you don't. Not until you get yourself a job you ain't going on vacation.

It's not a vacation. It's a business meeting to sign a contract to play in a basketball tournament.

Are you dense? Didn't you just hear me say this hustling stuff has to stop? You're thirty-six now, basketball ain't gonna work for you as a career if it ain't worked yet. We need stability, not more playtime. What about when those girls become teenagers, when they get ready to go off to school?

You're not listening to me. It's this thing setup by that Tex Randall guy, you know the one on the infotainment shows you watch? Billionaire, hangs out with all the celebrities, has that weird new cult, The Order.

Can't picture him, wait, did you just say cult? She threw her arms up and rubbed her face with both hands. Why you want to fuck around with a cult?

He scooted toward her, ready to hug her if she'd let him. She didn't let him. He said, It's good money. Said he'll pay me two hundred g's just for showing up. Just gotta fly out there first to sign the contract. To put all the details in order.

Shit, that is a lot of money, but your ass still needs to get a job, that shit won't last for forever.

There's opportunities for even more.

How so?

Well, if my team wins, we all get an extra hundred grand, and if I win MVP, we're talking so much money you might never need to work again, put our kids and their kids through college.

Sounds too good to be true. She stood up. Like she was done with the conversation and done with the show.

I think that's just how Tex Randall operates. Hey, where you going?

I don't like this. Seems like a lot of money to be throwing around on a basketball tournament.

Well, there is one catch.

On the last play of the half, The Rookie was double-teamed in the paint with two seconds left on the clock. He kicked a bounce pass through a mass of legs and out to Main Man in the corner, hit him right on the hands, the two guard drained the shot as the buzzer sounded, giving The Rookie his sixth dime to go along with sixteen points, eight boards and a block, on pace for a triple double. Big Daddy shook his head again, he'd done a lot of head-shaking in the first half, his hysteresis proving a counter to his desire for the Golden Dagger. His own stat line was a modest eight points, four rebounds, one assist, and two blocks. It was why his team looked forward to a modestly uphill battle in the second half, being down thirteen points.

He walked to the bench. The Refereed grabbed a cordless microphone and asked everyone, including the players, to remain seated for a short address by the Founder (the capital F was implied in the pronunciation). Tex stood up from his seat at center court, his oversized cowboy hat adding a larger than life appearance he might not have actually possessed. The same way his red sequined suit hid his humble Laredo upbringing, this man who could claim at least a modicum of truth to the rags-to-riches story, being a living example of how one can move from a farmhouse to a plantation home, although, admittedly, his father owned a rather large small farm, it wasn't exactly as meager as Tex made it out be. Tex grabbed the mic from The Referee and kissed him on the lips, then the two men bowed to each other.

He spoke into the mic, If I haven't greeted you personally, Welcome to Xibalba. We are halfway through our main event, our conclusion to the ceremonies and the precursor to the real festivities. We gather tonight for entertainment, true, but we should also not forget what this game is symbolic of. As we break for intermission, remember to consider how the descent into chaos restructures our lives to make a better future, a trophy we can hold with assuredness, symbolic of the game before the fall, the loss that must take place before any successes can be made. Tonight, we look away from a world that needs our structure to find the fractal organization of pure competition that exists self-similarly within that very same structure, to see it on a playing field where its arbitrariness can reveal how meaningless so many of our daily tasks are. I hope you have gambled bigly—he winked at the president who gave him a thumbs up—and gambled wisely, if that's your style. The thrill of victory will only make it that much more worth it. Even the crushing blow of defeat will be that much more bitter, in the ironic way that huge losses can be demonstrative of errors needing corrections on the way to a progressive agenda, one situated in the hands of those who actually have an ability to make progress. So let us now toss a prayer to our one and only true source of energy, a prayer to the Void.

Tex removed his hat, bowed his balding head, the crowd followed. Make me a channel of your ever-changing strength in the present moment. Make me stalwart about tradition in the face of reasonable prediction about the future. Make me a vehicle of a dogma that can't actually be dogmatic. Make me offer real choice packaged inside the illusion of a fake choice. Let me enjoy celebrating another's win. To the victor goes the spoils, and to the winner of the Golden Dagger goes the Ultimate Prize.

The crowd chanted, Truth. Truth. Truth. Truth.

Tex joined in their refrain. Truth. Truth. Truth. Truth. He put his hat back on. Raised his hand to silence them. And now, without further ado, here to sing our most famous psalm, please join me in welcoming Miley Cyrus. Tex listened to the applause and found it to his liking, found it to be good. In fact, it was just short of perfect. The only even minor annoyance was that Tom Cruise was absent, had rescinded his invitation. Tex tipped his hat once more at the singer who appeared on a rising stage at the end of the arena. The teams gathered their gear and headed towards the locker rooms as the singer went into a somewhat more solemn rendition of Wrecking Ball.

Big Daddy looked over his shoulder before entering the tunnel to see her humping a golden calf with a purple dildo. He thought about how life was a never-ending process of fake fucking your false gods into existence. He needed to ready himself to make his own empty sacrifice.

Remember it needs to be a free choice. With all the cards on the table, Tex said, handing the paperwork across his gargantuan oval desk, through the deer antlers that split the lamp. Then he asked, Did you talk to your wife about it?

Big Daddy grabbed the contract out of Tex's hand and said, Yeah. I talked to her. You got a pen? Where do I sign?

Tex picked up his Cartier Limited Edition and handed it across the table. He asked, What'd she say about it?

She told me not to do it. And then I told her I wouldn't try to win. He signed. We need the money, there wasn't a choice about it.

There's always a choice, but you're certainly not contractually obligated to try to win the Golden Dagger. Part of the experiment is asking the questions. How much is a life worth? Will the competition be greater or lesser because of the nature of the prize?

His eyes directed Big Daddy to the Golden Dagger on the end of his desk, stabbed into the top. He handed Big Daddy a check for fifty grand and said, As promised, your signing bonus. You'll get the rest after the game. Or your wife will get the rest should you be chosen.

You got a creepy way of saying these things.

I'd call it religious.

The religious are fond of murder, I'll give you that. Big Daddy thought about grabbing the contract back and ripping it to shreds but stopped himself. At least you're willing to put your money where your mouth is.

Tex showed his teeth before opening his mouth again. All money goes where your mouth is. We spend. We eat. We kill for more. We spend again. We eat again. That's the only difference between capitalists and ancient man. We threw in an extra step. So now we need a sacrament. A powerful sacrament. You know, human sacrifice has been an accepted practice in most cultures for most of history. Well, it still is, we just don't have a ceremony anymore. I'm only trying to make sacrifice spiritual again. Like I said, every player has a choice and I'm paying you well. Seems like you'd be a little more respectful of the hand that feeds you.

Is that a threat?

No. Just an observation.

Big Daddy stared at him. Then at the grandfather clock ticking behind him. Hey, can I ask you something? What the fuck is a Xibalba?

Good question. It's the Mayan underworld. They played a ballgame outside the gates to get in. Sacrificed the winners to an afterlife of endless suffering.

So you're a cultural appropriator too? Fucking white people man, y'all are so fucked up.

Sure we are. Sort of the whole point. I need something sufficiently voided of meaning. Sufficiently transparent. Sufficiently lampooned. People will only give you their soul if they can tell how empty your own is.

At halftime, Big Daddy sat in the locker room rubbing his temples. LuLu was talking to him, You need to use some more of them swim moves, man. That's how we beat these guys. Get that extra hundred.

Of course LuLu wanted Big Daddy to play better, to win the bonus money for the both of them. LuLu had no shot at the MVP, at being the spectacle after the spectacle. But the truth was Big Daddy did want it, all of it, not just the money and not just the trophy, but the warm embrace of eternal darkness too. It wasn't that he was suicidal or anything like that, just that the more he kept thinking about it since signing the contract, preparing himself should the worst (or best) happen, he had realized how much of his life was consumed by this continuous low grade suffering that only occasionally rewarded him with feelings of love or joy or warmth. It wasn't even the major shit either, just the boring shit like paying the bills and going to the bank that he could take no more. He knew for every hour of fulfillment he'd miss out on should he win, he'd miss out on another hundred mind numbing hours of daily minutiae. He would miss his girls, that was true, at least theoretically it was, he wouldn't really miss them where he'd be going, into the earth. Because this was the way out of all of it, the way to give them a future that wouldn't be as bleak as his own, hand them over a trust fund that wouldn't run out, let Tex mentor them in business. Generational wealth was the answer, buy a few of their own Congressmen. Start looking out for their own people. It was a beautiful dream, whether he would get to see it realized or not. It was worth being realized either way. First, he had some catching up to do. He said to LuLu, It was just a bad half. I'm gonna get this fucking money. I just need to call my wife first, you know, to get a chance to say, well, what it is I need to say.

Do what you got to do, Lulu said.

Ben Jammin, three-point specialist and two guard, their token white guy, as Homey, their small forward, liked to call him, which Big Daddy hated because maybe on the court Ben was an anomaly, but everywhere else he went, he was just another one of the pack. Ben said, We should probably take five for a quick meeting first, make a few adjustments, then you can call her.

Big Daddy said, No. I'm calling my wife first. Then we'll have a team meeting.

Fine. Don't listen to me.

Dude, everybody fucking listens to you all the mother-fucking time. Why don't you listen to somebody else every once in a while?

LuLu said, Hey now. No time for none of that.

Ajax spoke, Here here. Tipped back a Gatorade like a tall-boy. Force of habit, a habit that had kept Ajax out of the pros.

Big Daddy wondered if the sports drink were spiked now. He felt bad for Ajax, who was his favorite teammate, had the best heart, even if it were depressed by the booze half the time. Big Daddy rolled his head back over his shoulders, got up off the bench and walked away. Grabbed his phone out of his locker. He said, Hey Siri, call Cassandra.

Cassandra was in tears, I'm worried sick about you. Explain to me why I couldn't come with you.

Baby, It'll be okay.

Don't baby me. I could fucking lose you. Leave that place. We don't need the money.

He could feel her tears leaking out of the phone and drip-ping into his ear canal. It was an uphill battle. Maybe The Rookie would take it home anyway. He reassured her, Baby, I'm getting killed out there.

That's what I'm worried about.

No, I mean, this kid's too good for me. We'll just take the game check and put it in savings. It's gonna be okay.

Silence on the other end.

Baby?

Yeah, I'm here. I got a bad feeling. You need to go.

If I walk out at halftime, I'll be in a lot more danger than if I just lose. He squeezed the towel at his waist. Saying the words didn't sound right. He still wanted to win.

Be careful, please. What am I gonna tell our girls?

Tell them I love them.

Why don't you tell them that? They're right here.

No, no, wait. I don't need that right now. He looked over at the guys still sitting by the bench. I've gotta go. I'll see you in a couple days.

On his way back to meet his team, The Rookie poked his head into the locker room door. Said pssst, like in a sitcom or something—like he wasn't even a real life person.

Nobody knew where The Rookie came from. Only face none of them recognized on team selection day. Big Daddy thought The Rookie reminded him of himself at that age, if not for the fact that Big Daddy had still been on a high school ball team at that point in time, still thought of as a person with potential. They knew The Rookie wasn't an All-American, and no one had ever seen him in a Euro-league. Achilles claimed he was a foreigner, that he hid the accent well, why he didn't talk too much, because he didn't have the right paperwork. Dio, power forward for the kid's team, told them at the tryouts that he'd heard about some soft-spoken mammoth of a kid playing at Venice Beach who everyone said couldn't miss a thing, like it was magic or something. Main Man, who was fond of conspiracy theories, claimed The Rookie was so foreign that he was from another planet, which could have been as much the case as any other story, considering some of the rather extravagant and even non-human seeming audience members in attendance. Still, even though the rest of the players there were old friends and enemies, and despite seemingly every one of them having a different story to tell about the kid, Big Daddy doubted all of them. He just figured that every new talent always seems to come from a nowhere land, and every nowhere land's story is absurd the first time you hear it.

What you want, Big Daddy asked the kid.

Need to talk to you.

Why's that?

Cause, man, something 'bout the way you playing so far. Like you got too much to lose. Look, can we talk out in the hall?

Big Daddy followed him out the door.

The Rookie continued, It's like these forces beyond your control are trying to fuck you, you hear? And like, from me, it isn't like that, you get what I'm saying?

What do you know about anything I'm doing? Big Daddy put his hands on his hips. Fucking new guy.

You don't gotta be rude, dude. I'm here to make an offer.

What's that? Big Daddy turned around, began to crack the door. Didn't want to hear it.

I'll let you win. The Rookie said.

The second half was as lopsided as the first, only this time it was in Big Daddy's favor. Their team completed the comeback. The veteran found whatever motivation he'd been lacking and put up a twenty point fourth quarter. Couldn't be sure if the kid had lost it on purpose or not, he'd never agreed to the halftime deal, but getting to the hoop certainly wasn't the grind it'd been in the first half. Big Daddy wondered why the kid would play it this way. He didn't seem to be tanking in the first half. In any case, as LuLu dribbled out the final seconds on the clock, the crowd grew restless for the afterparty, throwing their won and lost money back and forth, half of them elated, the other half devastated. Whole corporations exchanged hands. Like how Adidas won the rights to Puma, permanently severing the already huge rift that existed in that family.

Tex grabbed the mic as everyone prepared to depart the arena for the fires on the South Lawn. I just want to say to both teams, Great game. I learned a lot. I hope everyone in attendance did too, players and crowd alike—he looked at Big Daddy—I don't think there could be anyone more deserving of this than you.

He held out the Golden Dagger, Big Daddy reached for it. Tex pulled it back. Not so fast, he said, we'll reconvene our services outside. Members of The Order, please find your ceremonial robes underneath your chairs. Now that the game is over, it's time for the celebration that brought us here. We'll have a sacrifice and a feast in about ten minutes.

On the South Lawn, in front of the bonfire, the Referee, still naked, except for a pair of bright blue kitchen gloves he was now sporting, gathered the players in a circle again, inside of more rings of concentric circles formed by the men and the couple of women who made up The Order. They wore their black and red robes with pride, ready to see the spectacle. Ready to feed themselves on truth.

Tex walked to the innermost circle, handed the Golden Dagger to the Referee, they kissed on the lips. The Referee grabbed Big Daddy. Brought him to the very center. Held the Golden Dagger pointed towards him. Yelled out, Are you ready to accept this award as recognition for all you have earned, as both a real and symbolic ending for the true story of your life?

The Rookie interrupted, stepped forward, Don't take him. Take me.

Tex spoke, We can't do that kid. Step back.

Big Daddy said, It's alright. I can handle it. Get going.

The Rookie said, But you're my old man.

Big Daddy saw the cleft in his chin, just like his own, but it couldn't be, was he old enough to have a kid this old?

The Rookie continued, Remember Tamara, you used to date her in high school?

A flood of memories rushed in, she'd moved to live with her grandparents across the country, in what seemed at the time like a brash move, but she never said why she had to leave her house. The Referee spoke, Kid, that's enough, step back. We have a sacrifice to attend to.

The Rookie stepped forward. Tex said, Just take them both.

Without hesitation, The Referee dropped the dagger on The Rookie in one fluid motion, pulled the knife back out, and then plunged it into Big Daddy's chest before The Rookie even hit his knees. Both men fell on their faces, sputtering blood from their mouths. Big Daddy feeling at the very end like this was the worst possible ending, like he'd have regretted it if he were still capable of feeling regret, to end up the victim in a white man's story, it was more typical than the setting warranted. He closed his eyes all the same and stopped breathing.

Tex yelled out, More meat for the meat eaters. The Order descended on the center, each member pulling a machete from underneath their robes. They moved in on the bodies, hacking at the limbs, disconnecting flesh from bone. They rubbed the meat with oil and then sprinkled it with salt from the buckets placed in another circle around the fire. They attached the flesh to metal spits and began the roast, praying to the eternal force of the market, to the Void. They heard the meat pop and sizzle. The aroma was almost indistinguishable from pork loin. Tex had his servants bring the wine in jugs, setting it at the members' sides.

When the meat was finished cooking, they ate with their hands, the flesh melting in their mouths, the forbidden flavor not washed away but only added to with the acidic taste of the wine. They looked forward to the whores, who were waiting inside Xibalba, like Tex had promised. They hoped it would all be good one day, this offensive game that could only be won by choosing the right kind of sacrifice, the kind that could represent what a life could mean and what a death could earn.

Orpheus to the White Sky

We don't know who to pray to anymore,
not without the clouds—we don't even know
how to keep hearing the roars of gastric thunder
which always signified your fierce hunger for more blood.
Now, just a clean buzz with occasional pop, zap,
ping, ping, ping. The sounds remind how
if it weren't for the bugs, we'd have no one left
to play these justice scales like steel drums.

I, for one, empty my spit valve, concentrating on
the moment I might break through the sulphuric dioxide,
the cover-up for the Night Sky, like an afghan
woven from threads of Fake News. O' how history spun
its yarns through the holes in the naive geo-engineers'
plans to provide in His absence. White
hardhats & white lab coats & white earpieces
extending from silver stethoscopes not listening to the cries

& so it was with my own tears for Mother Earth,
I, who had pledged to offer myself as a sacrifice
the whole time, I who'd become a Christ
in the next life, when the blood flow produced
by my own crown of thorns would reroute its course
inward, following the directions my Father

never bothered to take, toward the only other side
there is. Now my trumpet is a lullaby
for diminishing congregations & these
are not metaphors—

in this world, the sky
actually required our intervention, the sun too bright,
so overwhelmed we forgot how to die right & so left
to our own devices, we chose the most irreversible action
like a circle rounding out it's own form as a choke chain
by squeezing the breath out of a slender neck.

But it wasn't just us who could no longer inhale emptiness
when the rising coastlines & temperatures
had forced the population toward the poles,
when the food supply had gone from surplus to deficit,
when my own sweet wife was lost forever
in the Great Flood of '35, the diluvial generational moment,

our 9/11, our JFK Assassination, we had no other choice.
We turned the sky white & along with it,
everything else in sight. But that had been
an unintended consequence. True, we had known
it was risky, why we waited as long as we did,
always supposed to be a last ditch effort.

Did cool the planet, that part happened,
the way the heat got reflected off by the atmosphere,
but it also caused a luminescent & foggy glare,
the first time it rained, we noticed
how the lightning strikes were no longer pointed,
instead mere halos reflected in the newly clear ocean waters,
whole world a fluorescent bulb. No one
had the foresight to see how blue had always
framed our perceptions, that without it, the shapes faded,

and we were no longer a people, we were no longer the people,
we were no longer

        or I was no longer
standing at the end of the world hoping to find her
in the death of my Mother, blowing my horn for an audience
of half-life phonies, of real-time elitists, of anyone who
no longer had any ability to distinguish themselves.
It was there that the sweet music heard me extinguish
everyone else, like the last note of a symphony
eclipsing the horizon of a rock too silent by nature
to vibrate erosive inside the entropy of sound.

Judgment Day

The actor playing Seymour hit the note an octave too high, hiccuped, and then stopped. He looked out from center stage at the Miller Outdoor Theater, through the small auditorium, and up the expansive grass hill. The shadow figures behind the spotlight parted like the Red Sea. Families grabbed their ice chests and blankets, packed up, scattered across the hill. Seymour held a hand to his eyes. The band stopped playing. The special effects audio cut out. Audrey II, the plant, unzipped and opened. A sweaty man stepped out of the costume, which had proven even mustier than usual on an early spring night in Houston—where a Texas-sized summer could already be felt invading the borders, causing the more temperate season a crisis of identity. The puppeteer wiped his forehead with a bandana he'd pulled from the front pocket of his overalls, walked up next to Seymour and said, "What the fuck is going on out there?"

The houselights went up. A naked man alone on top of the hill. The people who'd paid for tickets in the seated area began to stand up and turn around, wanted to see what all the fuss was about. They wondered if they'd be getting a refund or not. Those sitting for free on the hill behind them had other worries. After a long pseudo-religious rant while stripping down, the naked man put his arms akimbo and went silent—a veneration to his own disruption. The crowd took one slow step backward at a time, a plodding recession away from his psychotically breaking center. He was macro-atomic, a radioactive half-life verging ever closer to toxic instability. He started ranting again, "Come here. I will show you the judgment on the great harlot who lives near the many waters. The kings of the earth have had intercourse with her, and the inhabitants of the earth became drunk on the wine of her harlotry."

He stared straight ahead at the stage, kept one hand extended toward the sky, brought the other down to his crotch. The actress playing Audrey stepped behind Seymour, as if the naked man were staring specifically at her. He began to masturbate furiously, shouting at the tops of his lungs, "Do you see the whore of Babylon? Do you see the whore of Babylon?"

A few men approached. The leader of the group yelled out, "Hey buddy. Stop that mess and put some pants on. There's kids here."

The naked man either didn't hear them or didn't care. He continued to stare straight ahead, kept on pumping his hand at his penis, yelling intermittently. The mothers shielded their children's eyes, well, those children who hadn't already been whisked away to the parking lot. When all these parents had told their kids they'd be taking them to see *The Little Shop of Horrors*, they hadn't meant it in any sort of a literal way.

One of the men who'd approached the naked man now kicked him in the knee. The naked man didn't cry out. He only fell down. They descended upon him, beating him with their fists until they were tired. By the time the officers who were stationed in the park had walked the winding path and made it all the way up the steep hill, the men had him tied up in a blanket serving as both restraint and covering. The officers asked what happened. The naked man spoke before anyone else could. "In her was found the blood of prophets and holy ones and all who have been slain on the earth."

His face was bruised, his lip split, he drooled a combination of saliva and blood. One of the cops looked at the group of men sternly. The leader said, "There's kids here."

The cop didn't respond. He looked at the other cop and said, "Guy's not in his right mind. We should take him down to West Oaks, let them deal with it. Be less paperwork anyway."

His partner said, "Looks pretty beat up to me. Maybe we should take him to a *real* hospital?"

The first cop said, "It ain't that bad. They got ice packs at West Oaks." He got down on his knee, pulled a pair of latex gloves from his breast pocket and put them on, flipped the man over, then put his knee to the man's back and began untangling him from the blanket. His partner put on his own set of gloves, reached down and handcuffed the naked man. Then, the first cop pushed the button on his walkie and spoke into his shoulder. "Yeah, we got us a *Cuckoo-for-Cocoa-Puffs* situation down at Miller Outdoor Theater, gonna need to take a perp into West Oaks. Might be a little late to changeover."

"Jesus, how many times do I need to go through this?"

"You don't need to do anything. But you came to me for help, and I can't help you if I don't know what's going on."

"But I've told you already."

"There's details that need ironing out."

"Okay, okay, whatever. So Titus and I were closing the bar at Griff's together that night. It was quiet for a Saturday. No crowd of barely-legals chugging down their last pitcher, the regulars weren't as drunk as regularly. We got out of there pretty quick, by like three a.m. at the latest. When we were locking up the gate, Titus asked if I wanted to come to his place to smoke a joint. I said sure.

"So we get back there, and there's all these like golden lamps and pentagram posters and this statue of a lamb with spears sticking out of it. I asked him what was up with the new decor. He tells me it's his Apocalypse Trip Spot. Then he tells me he doesn't have a joint. I laughed like he was bull-shitting me. He never didn't have a joint. He laughed too, said, 'Okay, you got me, I've got a joint, but I've also got this.' He dangled it in front of my face. I asked him, 'Is that what I think it is?'

"It was. Judgment Day. JD. The holy fucking grail. Stron-gest hallucinogen known to man. A gram of baby-blue powder staring me down from the other side of a translucent baggie, a whole other universe peaking through a rip in the space-time continuum. I couldn't believe it was really there. I couldn't believe it was really even real."

"What'd you call it? Judgment day? Don't think I've heard of it."

"Shit's rare, almost mythical, can only be extracted from one plant, the *Lupinus deum*, grows in just one valley in all of the Andes. The locals call it the Garden of the Forking Paths, say Borges named his story after it."

"Borges?"

"You never heard of Borges? What kind of a psychologist are you? He writes all these mind fuck stories, will twist your head up in knots, like an M.C. Escher painting or something."

"Doesn't ring a bell, but go on."

"Okay, but weird. So anyway, Borges used to make tea out of the leaves of the *Lupinus deum* and drink it in the morning before he wrote, they said it was where he got all those crazy ideas from. What we got was stronger than that. The shaman there have been boiling those leaves down into a paste for centuries, making this extract that can be smoked or ingested, and when you do, well, it's not so much that you have crazy ideas anymore but that you realize how your very existence is nothing more than a crazy idea. If that makes any sense at all. Anyway, we'd had an ear to the ground for JD for quite some time, maybe a decade even, been on some kind of Don Quixote-esque quest for the stuff, nothing doing. I thought it was all the product of stoner lore, that JD was just some imagined symbol for the highest of highs, but I seriously doubted we'd ever find the stuff. Titus was obsessed with it, though, used to spend half his free time reading stories on the internet from people who'd said they'd tried it. He'd ask random people in bars if they'd ever heard of it, usually to no avail, and even when they'd heard of it, it'd just be people like us who knew the legends but had never seen the evidence. Still, I wasn't exactly surprised when Titus turned up with it either.

"And then we weren't exactly tilting at windmills anymore. I asked Titus where he got it from. He said it just 'fell into his lap.' I asked if he'd planned on smoking it right then and there. He said, 'Shit, I ain't gotta wake up early tomorrow, do you?' I tried to mentally prepare myself. There were urban legends about people feeling like entirely different people after they smoked it, coming back fundamentally changed—which brings us back to right here and now."

"Just tell it to me like you're Stevie. Tell me what else you remember."

"Well, it could have been a dream."

"Sure, we've covered that possibility, but what it was is not what's important right now. I'm trying to get you to see something else. Will you just humor me?"

"Okay, okay. So Titus looks at me and says, 'I don't want to ruin anything, but be ready to lose your fucking mind.' Anyway, seemed like he'd already tried it. Kind of pissed me off."

"Why'd it piss you off?"

"Because, when I asked him about it, he told me 'acid [was] the kiddie ride at the amusement park compared to JD.' And then when I asked him how he knew that, he said he and Rebecca had done some a couple nights before when I was working the bar by myself."

"And you didn't want him to do it with Rebecca?"

"No, not after what had happened between the three of us."

"What happened between the three of you?"

"I don't want to get into the particulars right now, but like there's something personal about doing drugs together, like your best friend and your lady ain't supposed to be cutting you outta the party. And then they waited two whole days to say anything. It was suspicious is all."

"No, I get it. Just wanted you to clarify. So, when it was happening, you were already feeling upset?"

"I mean, yeah, I guess. But I was still curious too, you know? So I forgave him when he started the ritual. When he zipped his finger along the ziplock and delicately opened up the baggie. He took out a miniature spoon and scooped a small mound up, loading it into the narrow opening of a meth pipe. I must have looked nervous, because he said, 'What's the matter preacher's boy?' I told him it looked like we were smoking crack or something. He said, 'JD's all natural. Don't you trust me?'

"I answered with compliance. Titus put a butane torch to the side of the pipe. I watched it grow cloudy with vapors. Then, I put my mouth to it and hit it as hard as I could, as many times as I could, just like I'd been told to do, until I could hear 'a whistling from inside [my] own pituitary gland.'

"It tasted like shit. Like old man balls wrapped in rubber bands and tossed into a tire fire. I mean, real disgusting, still makes me want to vomit. But I powered through it, held back the urge to blow chunks. No pain, no gain, you know? Anyway, then I fell backwards into his ripped floral print couch, watched the gold lamps tilt in on each other, make the light look like a portal. Saw Titus stand up, jump into it, and disappear. Heard from the other side, 'Follow me.' When I got up, my knees locked, and I fell to the ground. Then I don't remember what happened. I woke up some time later, feeling all kinds of gross, on Titus' nasty-ass floor. I was yelling at the tops of my lungs, against my will, 'Dying is a game. Dying is a game. Dying is a game.' And then it just went black again."

Robert followed an orderly into the Day Room at the West Oaks Psychiatric Hospital, past the fake tree in the corner, through the prismatic light peeking through the blinds, and to a card table cater-corner to the tree where a strange woman wearing a red pantsuit sat, who the orderly informed him was supposed to be his wife. She jumped up when she saw him and gave him a hug. She said, "Oh my God, what happened to your face?"

He assumed she meant the bruises, but the question had caused him to think about the first time he'd gone to the mirror at the hospital just yesterday. When he'd expected to see a round bald head, he saw instead a mop of thick black hair hanging just above a set of high chiseled cheek bones. His blue eyes were brown. His ears, which normally sported a set of zero-gauge plugs, remained unpunctured. His scraggly beard was also a thing of the past (or the non-past or the never-was, whatever you could call this confounding state of affairs).

The woman in the red pantsuit grabbed his arm gently, interrupted his thoughts, "Are you okay? I've been worried sick about you. Oh Robert, what happened?"

Hearing his name startled him once more. Although the orderly had informed him earlier that morning about his true (or truer?) identity, he remembered being a man named Stevie, a bartender dialectician, as he liked to call himself, seeing his central task as offering a talking cure to his hard-living and often run-down clientele. To do that, he derived his knowledge from wisdom in books held at the library for free that suckers paid thousands of dollars to read at universities. He also remembered being a man that liked to take a lot of drugs. In fact, his last memory was at his friend Titus' house, on some crazy shit called JD, Titus glowing like Zeus, the Greek God himself, thunderbolts and stars coming from the palms of his hands. When people had told him JD could produce born again experiences after you came back down, this was not what he'd thought they'd meant.

"Do you know who I am? I'm told you're having problems with your memory."

He tried to think harder. He wanted to tell her something, not because of the teary eyes that seemed longing, but because of the grimace she couldn't hide, the personal offense she'd taken to his clear lack of recognition. He continued to remain silent, figured it was his best option at the moment.

"Did you take something, like drugs?"

"No?" He finally spoke, a reaction, sounded more like a question to her question than an answer. He wondered if she'd noticed. He could keep denying, especially since he wasn't really sure that he had taken anything, he could have just gone crazy (was this what they meant by crazy), how he'd concocted a new set of memories. All explanations were still on the table, but he wasn't planning to advertise himself as a drug user. In a hospital like this, addicts were the lowest of the low, condescended to even more than the schizos.

"I'm sorry. I didn't mean to accuse you. I'm just glad you're safe."

"I'm sorry. I wish I could figure this out, but I'm just—"

"Oh honey, it's okay." They were still standing, she gave him another hug, he made the red of her pantsuit maroon with his tears. After he'd collected himself, they sat down at the table. She said to him, "Everything's fine. The nurse at the front desk said they'll run a series of tests and try to figure out what happened to you. You'll probably need to be prepared to stay for at least a week. I've got Doug handling all your business. You just try to relax and get better."

When she said the name Doug, a face popped into his head, a wrinkled face with glasses, his partner, ten years his senior, taught him everything he'd ever known about real estate. He looked back at the woman in the pantsuit. He said, "Betty?"

"That's an encouraging sign."

A film clip ran through his head, meeting her at one of his fraternity's parties in college, she was a member of their sister sorority. She still sometimes told the joke, "You know what they say when Alphas and Lambdas get together?" It didn't have a punchline. Oh, how it irritated him. Yes, she really was his wife. He remembered the night he proposed, fresh off landing his first big boy job out of grad school, a marketing exec at Intuitech, a software firm. He took his first paycheck to Zales and spent it all on a gigantic diamond. Did he really love her, he wondered now, her picture was becoming clearer but no warmth was necessarily attached to it, he remembered only that the idea of her seemed to bode well for his aspirations, a smart, attractive woman to introduce to associates, it'd been a successful marriage on that front. But he must have loved her on some level, he thought, as memories continued to flicker like sixteen millimeter, the scare when she'd been in a more *traditional* hospital than this one a couple of years back, from a case of pneumonia that had gotten past bad, at her worst, she was running a one hundred six fever, coughing and gurgling on what seemed like an infinite loop, the doctors had even prepared him for the possibility he might lose her, one of her lungs had collapsed, he had been worried to his core, about her, about his daughters, about more than how it might have looked for his career, that much was true, but if he were being honest, his career was certainly one of his worries too, how he would find the time to make money if he'd have to raise his daughters by himself. It was a quite robust career, he had to admit, he thought about all he had accomplished since she'd recovered, just last year *Forbes* had ranked his and Doug's real estate firm as one of the one hundred most profitable businesses in the country, they were number sixty-seven to be exact, a modest ranking they actually preferred to one of the top spots, because Houston, the place where they lived and did the vast majority of their business, was the biggest modest city in the country. Sixty-seven was a ranking that would play favorably to their future growth factors.

The film clip stopped suddenly. His head started to throb when the instinct of number crunching collided with an inability to predict what the future might hold. He folded his arms and put his head on the table. There was this growing feeling that he had wasted his life, but he couldn't tell if the negativity were coming from himself, as Robert Lannigan, or if this were a part of Stevie, who was still in there somehow, fighting for his own sense of selfhood. He heard his wife speak again, "Honey, talk to me. What's going on with you? You're never this quiet."

"Tell me more about Rebecca. How did you meet her?"

"Rebecca? Why do you want to know more about her?"

"She seemed to mean something to Stevie."

"She meant something, that's true. But like, shouldn't we be talking about Robert, about why he's got this set of memories that don't belong to him?"

"Memories are really nothing more than the raw data of the stories we tell about ourselves to ourselves. I'm just trying to help you turn that data into information, so it can be used productively. It'll let you think about it easier if you just let it flow out. So tell me like you're Stevie. It doesn't so much matter what I think, but what you think. Maybe you'll find a resolution to Stevie's story that Robert can live with, extra memories or not."

"Whatever. Luckily, Robert's got a lot of money to waste on you."

"So? Rebecca?"

"Well, Rebecca, she didn't like labels, I thought I didn't

either, but after dating her—sorry—it's always so complicated to explain, for the sake of parsimony, she was basically my girlfriend. But we were going for that whole Sartre and De Beauvoir sort of thing, you know?"

"No, I don't. Your references are a bit obscure, no?"

"Sartre and De Beauvoir are not obscure. What kind of a quack school did you go to?"

"The kind that makes me your only option."

"Okay, I'm sorry. That was uncalled for. Sartre and De Beauvoir were existential French philosophers and lovers. Never got married or anything. Together because they chose to be together, because they enjoyed their time together, because they respected each other, they didn't feel the need to live together, had other partners on occasion, essentially, they could understand each other enough to realize no one person could be the end all be all for anyone else, who else can boast of a love that deep? That's what Rebecca and I were going for.

"I met her at the park outside of The Menil. It was sunrise, and Titus and I were enjoying the last wave of a mushroom trip that had started some hours earlier. We were smoking a joint, watching the trees breathe, the dew hanging like our extra-extended adolescence in the humidified air. She was walking her dog, in the middle of her morning routine before she would teach a class for her assistantship at U of H. Her head was bright and bald, shaved with a Bic, it appeared. I said to Titus, 'Look, it's my twin.' He said, 'Man, if she had a twin, her and her twin still might not make one of you.' I looked down at my belly poking out of my holy t-shirt and laughed. In fact, we both laughed harder than we should have at that joke, rolling on the ground like children. The grass had been cut recently and was stuck to our sweaty arms. Rebecca walked up and asked to hit our joint. She was wearing a Sonic Youth t-shirt. I thought to myself that she had tastes. She said, 'You two look like you're having fun.' Then she asked us what we were on, if we could get anymore of it, and if she could have some."

"Her dog hopped up on me. Must have spooked me because she told me not to worry, that he wouldn't bite. Told me to call him by his name, Anubis. I normally love dogs, but when I'm tripping, something about being around animals, like I feel like they can see through the pathetic veneer of how I present myself to the world, like they seem to disapprove of the very material that created my soul. But it was her dog, and Rebecca had an aura around her that made me want to be better. I called out to the dog, managed to pet his head without freaking out too much, until he licked me and I threw myself backwards. She asked again if I was okay. I figured I should defend myself, especially if she'd already found us out. 'Sorry, it's just the mushrooms,' I said. She said, 'Mushrooms. I knew it,' and then she asked for my phone. I handed it to her without thinking about it. She put her number into my contacts, told me not to forget her name, said she put the middle finger emoji next to it to remind me. Told me we should do mushrooms together sometime.

"And then we did mushrooms together, about a week later, exploring each other's bodies like children playing doctor, with this keen sensitivity that was as asexual as it turned excessively sexual when we fucked like possessed spirits later that night. In neither phase did we really talk that much, the pleasure was too overwhelming, we didn't really know anything about each other, except for what we were learning were the right parts to touch. People want to say falling in love should be about this full connection with another person's mind, body, and soul, but for us, we fell in love instantaneously, and it was purely physical, like we first had to write the scripts on each other's bodies through an observed performance so we could later come to find personalities in each other.

"I guess what I'm trying to say is that pleasure was the foundation of our relationship, which made sense considering we both lived semi-hedonistic lifestyles, hers a bit more ambitious than mine, but yeah, our sex life was the ground on which a true partnership began to take root. Those first six months, it was like we were teenagers again, my thirty-five year old body found a vigor I hadn't had in over a decade. We fucked like five times a day. Of course, I don't want it to sound like I'm bragging here, being salacious for no cause, it's just that what people usually refer to as sordid details generally speaking shouldn't be thought of as sordid, nor are they just details. Often, they're the driving force of the story, even if they aren't told. I'm just trying to be up front about it.

"Our sexual compatibility opened us up for other levels of comfort with each other. I eventually felt safe telling her my feelings because first I had told her how I wanted to be spanked, and she bought a black paddle with a pink heart on it, surprised me with it. I came to desire her inner being because first she had figured out this trick with her tongue, putting it on my outer being, creating inside me a sense of the divine. And I came to feel I needed her in my life after feeling comfortable enough to confess that I'd wanted to be fucked with a strap-on, and after she'd delivered, my prostate felt as good about choosing her for a lover as my soul did, which admittedly, also felt quite jovial.

"But I'm not trying to make it sound like she was just some sexual object. She'd tell you, if she could, that she got plenty from me too. I don't fit in many places, and aside from intellectual prowess, I've never had much else going for me, but I have always been a quite generous lover. It's part of my ethos. Also, I could tell it the other way around, tell you first about how much I came to respect her as a fully-formed person, which was true, but it was my body that told me first, like it had senses we haven't found words for yet, like it was the thing that told me she was the one (or whatever) with enough force that it wouldn't allow my normal psychic anxieties to talk me out of being vulnerable around her.

"I was happy my body was right. She was a great conversationalist, both as a speaker and a listener, and she never judged me. She valued my curiosity, because she had her own deep curiosity for life. Not to mention the more everyday parts of our relationship found an adequate complement as well.

"Our record collections were almost identical, which made it easy to find background noise to our getting to know each other. At the time, we were listening to The Flaming Lips on an almost daily basis. Then, there was the fact that she was an artist, and I saw art as the only human ambition worth bothering yourself over. I even genuinely liked her work, a lot of mixed media collage type stuff, her favorite artist was Rauschenberg. And she was fond of reading like I was fond of reading, even the same genres, the obscure philosophy and the most sesquipedalian of literary fictions, she was comfortable next to me while we both had books open, consequently, she knew how to think, and she knew how to share silence, which might have been the most important part of our relationship in the end.

"So yeah, what you were asking earlier, did she mean something to me? I fucking love that girl. We were together as not-together for four years, she would give me hell if she knew I'd been counting. But I miss the shit out of her."

Robert shoveled forkfuls of bone-in rib eye covered in melted blue cheese into his smacking, mostly-opened gums. He wasn't even waiting for one bite to go down before he just jammed the next one in there. Blue cheese dripped down the unkempt beard he'd been growing since he'd been out of the hospital. It was like he'd never been to Fleming's before, even though it was he and Betty's favorite restaurant.

He downed a three-fourths full glass of Far Niente

Cabernet before picking up the bottle and draining the rest into his oversized glass. He held up the empty high above the table, motioned to the waiter across the room, pointed at the bottle. Then he took another titanic swell of a swig.

"Slow down honey," Betty said to him. She was wearing her favorite low-cut black dress tonight. They hadn't had sex since he'd been back, and he'd guessed his wife had intended to rectify that situation sooner rather than later.

"Sorry. Just this shit is fucking good." He took another sip.

"It's Far Niente. Of course it's good. Would you stop swearing?" She took a sip out of her own glass and picked at her salmon with her fork, not moving any of the fish toward her mouth. She looked sick all of a sudden.

He said it again. "I'm sorry."

"Jesus, Robert. Why are you apologizing? Ever since you disappeared, something's different."

He didn't respond. He thought about the dream—or the coma? The hallucination? Maybe the booty juice—as his roommates at the hospital had called it—the drugs they'd used when he'd arrived in a state of hysterics, the part he still couldn't remember as Robert or as Stevie—but that giant syringe they'd slammed into his ass—might have had some lasting effect on him. He wondered if it was where Stevie came from? But then again, he'd had plenty of time for those drugs to wear off, and he still felt more like Stevie than like Robert.

But as bad as the dislocation felt, it wasn't what was bothering him so much at the moment. He looked across the table at his wife's perfect curls, at her lipstick, at her necklace, at her press on nails. How did anyone fall in love with a woman who tried that hard? And how did he consign himself to the rest of his life with her?

The waiter brought the wine and ended the uncomfortable silence. He held out the Far Niente on a golden linen. Popped the cork and poured a small sample into Robert's glass, waited for him to approve. Robert stuck his hand up and shook his head. "Just fucking pour it already."

Betty didn't say anything this time. She just waited for the waiter to pour a glass before she drained the majority of it. Gave Robert the stink-eye as she swallowed. The waiter walked away.

Robert said, "What's wrong with you?"

"Seriously Robert? You disappear for three days, turn up in a mental hospital, of all places, can't remember your name or where you were or what you were doing, come home, spend day and night on the internet, haven't been to work since I don't know when, you're daughters can't figure out what the fuck's wrong, now you're embarrassing us in public, and you're going to ask me what's wrong with me?"

"Okay, okay. I'm sorry. I don't want to fight. I'm just, well, adjusting still."

"I'm sorry too. But come on, how long is this supposed to take, and could you at least try to pretend like you're having fun? I am your wife." She grabbed her glass and lifted it to Robert. "To putting this whole mess behind us."

"What mess?"

"Oh, drink up."

They clinked glasses and both finished the rest of what was left. Robert then poured the rest of the bottle between them and motioned to the waiter for another one. They finished dinner without speaking, ordered another bottle for dessert. The candlelight grew brighter as their mutual buzz grew more disdainful. They killed the dessert bottle and decided to stay for one more, still barely speaking. Just drinking, like they were in an absurdist version of a Raymond Carver story, where the other couple is in attendance by way of their absence, *What We Don't Talk About When We Don't Talk About Love*, they killed that bottle and ordered one more, promised the maitre'd they'd use a Lyft to get home. Robert gave him his keys to hold on to. Slouching into their chairs, struggling to sit-up, they kept on drinking like they were escaping the wrath of a former lover, like they were trying to out-forget each other.

"Did I tell you about the time Titus and I got pulled over with seventy five thousand dollars in cash?"

"No, can't say that you did."

"So, before I got Titus on at Griff's as a door guy, he'd been working for this ATM company, they'd go around to convenience stores and try to get them to replace whatever perfectly fine machine they had with the highfalutin machine his boss was installing, a faster network speed and compatibility to more kinds of cards. Said they gave the store owners a higher share of the profits too, but who knows what's actually true in business? Anyway, part of Titus' job was to stock the ATMs they already had with cash, so he often carried around shitloads of it, which meant he needed a gun, just in case. Like everything else with Titus, he couldn't carry just any gun, it had to be the biggest one you're legally allowed to carry, in this case, some semi-automatic pump action snub-nose shotgun, he'd shown me how it all worked when he got it, but I couldn't tell you what brand or anything, I've never really been a gun guy. As you well know, I get sad sometimes, was no different then, and I don't trust myself enough not to blow my brains out some night when I've had too much to drink.

"Anyway, I'm getting off track, making myself sad now, and this is supposed to be a funny story. So aside from the gigantic gun, Titus had also lost his wallet one night when we'd ended up doing a bunch of blow after leaving the bar and he hadn't yet replaced his ID. Then there was the fact that we were carrying a gigantic baggie full of white, unmarked pills, which weren't really illegal, they were Viagra, or the generic equivalent, and true, you were supposed to have a prescription to buy them, but they weren't scheduled as a controlled substance or anything."

"So, why were the two of you cruising around with a baggie full of Viagra?"

"Oh, well that's the funny part. About a month earlier, Titus slept with this girl Veronica we all knew, who, well, I'm not judging or anything, but she was known as the Skank by more than one of the regulars at the bar. Personally, I thought she was cool, always tipped well, who gave a shit how many people she slept with? But like I think it got into Titus' head, because in all honesty, it was kind of a lot of dudes, not that there's anything wrong with that, but it's effect on him was not good. So Titus sleeps with her, the next day he goes to take a leak and blood comes out. We were at work when it happened. He came up to me where I was washing beer glasses in the sink, let out a slew of words I won't repeat here about Veronica, then said he had to leave, felt bad about it being a Friday night, how we'd be short, but that 'you can't fuck around with stuff down there,' and if I had a problem with him leaving early, I should blame Veronica.

"Turns out, though, the asshole had a kidney stone. Had nothing to do with Veronica. His blood work came back negative for anything else. As far as I know, he never apologized to her for spreading all that shit around about her."

"I'm sorry to interrupt, but can I ask you something?"

"Sure."

"I don't know. From our conversations, you seem like a smart guy, and a nice guy, why would you hang around with someone like that?"

"Man, Titus and I have known each other since longer than we remember knowing each other. Our dads are best friends, or last time I checked anyway, but we were raised together. My father was a preacher and his father was the music director at our church. It was one of those stupid mega-churches where all they talk about is how much money God rewards the faithful with, the preacher most of all. But yeah, Titus can be a better guy than I'm describing him. Maybe I'm just airing the dirty laundry because last time I saw him I was pissed at him."

"You were pissed at him?"

"Yeah, but let me finish the funny story first."

"Okay, go ahead."

"So like I said, turns out he just had a kidney stone when he thought he had an STD, but like after he passes the kidney stone, like the scare from sleeping with Veronica did something to him. So he starts dating this girl Roxy, who he'd been chasing around for forever, he was excited, after they'd been dating a couple weeks, he keeps telling me he has a good feeling, like he might want to make her his girlfriend, like she might be for real, for real, the one. She didn't turn out to be, but it felt genuine at the time. Anyway, Roxy and Titus try to sleep together for the first time, and he can't get it up, all this pressure and worry created a mental block, and he was afraid she would think it was an ongoing problem. So with two scares in a row, on complete opposite sides of the spectrum, he's thinking he'll never have another meaningful sexual experience again, so he calls our friend Beetle, who can get damn near anything, usually within the hour, and sure enough Beetle came through, with more dick pills than anyone could or should use in a lifetime.

"So to recap, we're in his truck, we've got a backpack in the backseat filled up with dollar, dollar bills, lots of them, a gigantic semi-automatic shotgun, a baggie full of dick pills, and Titus didn't have his license to drive with him. Not to mention that I had brought a roadie along, a Bloody Mary, so spicy it'd make you see God if you took a big enough sip. We had weed on us too, but that wasn't anything out of the ordinary, we always had weed on us, it was a given. Anyway, Titus, knowing all this, runs a solid red light anyway, right in front of a cop car.

"The cops, there were two of them, smell the weed right away, pull us out of the car, they toss my drink, a shame, it was a good drink. They ask us for ID, but only I had any. One of them looks into the rear window of Titus' truck and sees his gun, then he puts handcuffs on Titus, marches us both back to behind his cruiser while his partner searches the truck. He pulls out the gun first, which was already loaded, as it turned out, the cop had to eject a round from the chamber. That was not legal. Then, he goes back into the car, and he finds the duffel bag Titus had the cash in. He opens it so his partner can see, his eyes all wide, his posture perked up, thought he caught himself a couple of big-time dealers, like he might have a chance to put dope on the table on the evening news. His partner, who was standing with us, said, 'Looks like you boys are in for a long night.' I thought so too when I saw his partner walk around to the other side of Titus' truck and find the baggie full of pills. Luckily, they seemed to forget about the weed.

"Titus said to the cop standing with us, 'I can explain all of it. Can I call my boss first?' The cop says, 'Why don't you just explain first?' The other cop walked back over to where we were standing. Titus tells them about his job as an ATM contractor, then he tells them how he lost his license, and then he tells them the gun is registered and legal, and then he tells them the pills are just Viagra. And the cops buy all of it, seem to believe him straight out of his mouth. They let Titus call his boss. The boss comes down, gives Titus shit about bringing a friend along for his runs but verifies that the cash is company cash and destined for an ATM a half mile away. Meanwhile, one of the cops used a drug kit on one of the pills and it didn't check out for anything illegal. They let us go with a warning, after all that, didn't hurt that we were a couple of white dudes, I suppose. But it still just cracks me up to think of Titus standing there telling these two cops how he needed dick pills because he couldn't get it up for the girl of his dreams. Anyway, I guess it'd be funnier if you knew Titus."

"I'm not sure he'd be somebody I'd want to know. What was it like when y'all were growing up together? What kind of trouble did the two of you get into then?"

"I don't really want to talk about my childhood. I don't feel like crying."

"Robert! Robert! Why can't my laptop find our network?" Betty yelled from the top of the stairs. He was in his study with the door opened, clicking his mouse, eyes darting. He didn't even look up from the screen, just yelled back. "Oh, sorry. I set up a security feature. You have to search for the name of the network manually when you want to connect."

"That's a pain in the ass."

"It's necessary. For privacy."

That's why they call it a Very Private Network, he thought to himself. She put her hands on her hips, turned around to walk back to the bedroom, stopped, and then turned back toward Robert. "Are you doing something illegal?"

"No. Just can't ever be too careful."

When he first got out of the hospital, lying to his wife was difficult, but he was getting more comfortable with it. This time he wasn't technically lying. True, putting up a VPN was a way of disguising yourself when you downloaded Tor—a browser for searching the deep web—true, it was something that could get you placed on a federal watchlist if they knew you were doing it, and true, converting large amounts of cash into Bitcoin was frowned upon and could get you audited by the IRS, but none of it was technically illegal either, provided you didn't use the technology for illegal purposes, which was, granted, hard to do since half of the .onion sites were kiddie porn or drug markets, and because Robert was, in fact, looking for drugs—or, rather a specific drug, JD. He hadn't found it yet, nor had he purchased anything else that would be considered a felony. He was still in the clear on the legality front, aside from the small amount of marijuana he'd purchased, which wouldn't even get you charged in the county these days, had to be more than four ounces to catch a case. It didn't matter though. He didn't need any further excuses to justify what he felt he needed.

Betty disappeared back into the bedroom. She either believed in his lawfulness or didn't feel like arguing. He was fine with either possibility at the moment. He just wanted to be left alone. He had to find the JD. Nothing else was helping him to sort between the two lives that occupied this one life, or what seemed like two lives, or however it was he was supposed to explain it to himself.

Anne walked into his office. He closed his browser. She said, "Dad. Are you going to come watch me play tomorrow? We get into State if we win."

There was a time when his daughter's softball games were the one thing more important to him than money, but lately, he just couldn't handle the crazy parents—even though he used to be one. Was he still one? Was he crazy?

"Dad?"

"Sorry. You know I haven't been feeling well." He stood up from his desk, bent down and tried to give her a hug. She didn't return it. He said, "Look, I'll try. But I won't make any promises."

Anne rolled her eyes and walked out without saying anything else. They all hated him here. He sat back down at the desk and reopened Tor. He had a message in an encrypted inbox from a user named BEETLEG364. Robert had reached out to the guy first. Remembered Titus' friend Beetle, figured it was a sign. Anyway, it wasn't the same Beetle, or at least, this one didn't know anyone named Titus, which was odd. Didn't seem like even in a city as big as Houston you could find two drug dealers who went by Beetle. The message said, "Might have a line on some JD. Can you meet in person anywhere?"

Robert tried to think of a place where nobody knew him.

He wrote back, "Ever been to Griff's?" He hit send. Now, it was time to wait.

He sat back in his chair. Betty came into his office. Slammed the door behind her. She said, "Are you happy?"

It seemed like a loaded question. But momentarily, he was tired of lying to her. "No, in fact, I'm not happy. I'm not happy at all. But I'm seeing the fucking shrink. Just like you asked."

"Don't give me that. Your daughter's crying. Wonders why you hate her. Can you go fix it?" She pointed her thumb over her shoulder, toward the door of his office, presumably she meant Anne's bedroom.

Robert shrugged his shoulders. Leaned further back in his chair. "What do you want from me?"

Betty clenched her fists, like she was maybe thinking of starting a physical altercation. She yelled, "I don't want anything. It's not about me. You've got a daughter in there who loves you and maybe needs some attention every once in a while. Ever think of that? You self-centered motherfucker."

"Stupid bitch!"

"What?!"

Robert was on his feet now, walking past her. He said in a monstrously calm voice, "You called me a name first. I'm getting out of here."

Betty put her hands on her hips. "You're going to your daughter's game tomorrow."

"I'll go wherever I want to go." He opened the door to his office, exited the room.

"I guess that means the bar again," he heard as he was walking out the front door.

"You ever worry about being an elitist?"

"No. I figure such labels are mostly used as insults by the ignorant and the envious. I mostly ignore the whole concept."

"Yeah, I never put much stock into it. Like who wants

to be normal? I mean, I don't think I was an elitist either, I avoided traditional education like the plague, or traditional anything really, but like Rebecca, she said she thought I was an elitist. She told me, 'It's not a matter of status, it's a matter of attitude.' I told her that as far as I saw it, the word elite implied a connection to a tradition, that it was a person who is interested in an institutional hierarchy, a person like herself, who had just graduated with an MFA, who might be considered an elitist. I didn't mean to give her the rub about her education all the time, but sometimes I couldn't help myself.

"She said, 'Have you ever considered maybe you're an elitist by the way you construct moral hierarchies?' I asked her what she meant by that. She rolled her eyes and said, 'You're always talking about who's in the A group and who's in the B group, and then you and Titus with your...' She started to mock me. '... give me your Mt. Rushmore of American Punk Acts from the 1980s.' Then, she informed me that Mt. Rushmore was built by a fucking Klansman, on territory that was straight up stolen from the Lakota, who all call the thing Mt. Crazy Horse. After that, she went low, told me I was like my father, the preacher, said I had 'one of the most religious outlooks on life' of anyone she knew. I consider myself a fervent atheist, so I initially took offense, but then she told me, 'When everything's sacred, there's no room for a concept of reality.'

"I mean, it hit me where it counted. I got what she was saying. I knew I was a bit of a snob, but I also knew I mostly stayed the fuck out of everyone else's way. Kept to my little square mile radius of places I hung out at in the Montrose. I drank my beers, tended bar, and read lots of books. Took the occasional mind altering substance. I didn't drive. I didn't own a car. I shopped locally. I only ate at privately owned restaurants, when I even went out to eat. Most of the time I cooked, with food I bought at Canino's on Airline."

"What's Canino's on Airline?"

"It's a little farmer's market over in Heights Proper,

independently owned and operated, all private seller to private purchaser."

"Oh yeah. I've heard of that place. It's in a nice area. Has lots of potential."

"That's what Robert would think."

"Well, you're supposed to be Stevie right now."

"Yeah, yeah, I know. It was just a joke. But for real, like maybe the people who lived there before liked the area enough already before all the white people like me moved in. I guess Canino's is doing the best business they've ever done, but I also keep waiting for them to sellout to some schmuck developer— like myself, I suppose. Anyway, getting back to the whole initial point with Rebecca and elitism, and her accusing me of trying to construct moral hierarchies, like I did a lot to avoid becoming a part of the capitalist machine, and it was hard work, like that shit is ubiquitous, you can't really ever escape it, all you can do is try your best to vote with your dollar, I don't have any faith that a real revolution would ever happen, so what else is there, and like most people don't even fucking care that you take the time to do even that much, which is so not enough, and so you always feel like Sisyphus, and then on top of that, these same people call you things like a fucking elitist. So yeah, I was a bit miffed at first when she said it.

"But then I thought about it. Like the premise of what she was saying, that I claimed to have this whole optimistic nihilistic approach to the world, this whole embrace your own emptiness to find the freedom by which you can be happy, and I was never all that happy. All I knew how to do was to hunt for pleasurable experiences to make all the moments of worrying about the world's problems go away. And then she also sort of pointed out how part of the reason I could live the way I did was because I was white, that I'd likely be in jail because of my lifestyle if I wasn't white, and how, at least at an institution, she had the ability to open doors for some students who weren't like herself.

"So like Rebecca and I talked it out, we both decided that maybe we both had a point, that she could benefit from imagining what her artistic life would look like without having to think about how it fit into the academy's conversation or what value that conversation placed on the material value in dollars and cents of the actual media she produced. And I could use a little hanging out with the common man to find the inherent goodness that's inside of all people. Rebecca suggested we go to this folk art festival thing they were doing on the steps of city hall. It was all this rah, rah, America bullshit, all these people hocking American flag paintings and American flag sculptures and American flag t-shirts, and well, you get the idea. Basically, it was a place we were both supposed to hate, but we promised ourselves we'd try to have a good time.

"So, we went to a costume store and bought old glory workout gear and Uncle Sam top hats. We drank Cokes on the way there, the quintessential American product, good for two sips and then hot and awful the rest of the way down."

"Tastes better in Mexico too."

"Ha. Yeah. Never thought of that. Anyway, when we got to the festival, we got our faces painted with American flags. We drank cheap domestic beer, and we talked to people wearing MAGA hats, tried to ask them ways that we could come to agree on anything politically, mocking their accents after we'd collected their answers and they were safely away, the best one we heard was about how the president should stay off Twitter. At one point, I said to her, 'Aren't we doing right now what we came here to avoid doing? Like we're ironically enjoying this festival, which is a way of saying we're better than these people, and also sort of a way into enjoying these people objectively, as forms of entertainment for our own pleasure. Isn't that what elitists do?'

"Rebecca said, 'The first step to truly enjoying something is to ironically enjoy it.'

"I said, 'But don't we also want to avoid enjoying mask-on Nazism unironically? Or even ironically?'

"She said, 'Well, okay, I guess you have a point there, but look, the Trumpers are just one part of this. Mostly, it's just good old fashioned American fun, like that hot dog eating contest. Most of these people probably don't give two fucks about any kind of politics.'

"She was right, the majority of the crowd were just there to celebrate freedom, and thought all the talk of politics was preventing them from doing so, and she was also right that the hot dog eating contest was quite impressive. Joey Chestnut showed up. Ate fifty-five dogs, which wasn't close to his own record, he probably didn't train as hard with it being a charity event, but it was still totally disgusting and impossible to look away from, in a good way. You'd be amazed at the crowd energy during a spectacle like that. It made the whole thing worth going to, for sure.

"Something else of note happened there too, like unrelated to elitism or patriotism, we met a woman named Cecelia. She was selling these wood carvings, and Rebecca asked her if she could use any of them in her collages. Cecelia agreed. Rebecca bought all of them. When she was cashing us out, I accidentally bumped the table and knocked over her margarita, which came in a super skinny tall glass to give the appearance of being a larger drink than it actually was. I offered to buy her a new one, departed for the margarita truck and left her and Rebecca alone for a few minutes. When I came back, Rebecca pulled me aside and asked if we could bring Cecilia home with us."

"Home with you?"

"About that, so Rebecca and I had been bickering more often and sleeping together less often. It wasn't a drastic enough problem yet for me to worry about the status of our not-quite-a-relationship relationship, but enough for me to bring it up with her. We decided we wanted to spice things up as a way of generating excitement and closeness, and both of us were curious about what it would be like to live a polyamorous lifestyle. Rebecca was also curious about being with another woman. But we weren't exactly sure how to approach the situation. Nobody talks about these kinds of things in public. Anyway, we came to the conclusion that if we were out and about, had a good enough buzz (we certainly did by the late afternoon when we met Cecilia), and if the idea arose naturally, we'd try to do a threesome, to stick our toes in the water. It had been a conversation we'd had months earlier, and then it just sort of came to fruition that day.

"Anyway, I asked Rebecca how and why she had asked Cecilia, and she said she just asked her straight out, without much thought, felt comfortable around her, was just honest about what she wanted. We hung out with Cecilia at her table until the end of the festival, and I also found her quite charming, inviting. She had all the warmth of a Southern belle without the stuffy repressive outlook on life. She said to me at one point, 'You know, these people here, and I say this with love, cause these are my people, but they'd be a lot happier if they had a little more marijuana in their lives and a little less Jesus. Speaking of, you got any reefer?'

"I loved that she called it reefer. We smoked a joint in my car, and we rocked out to *Exile on Main Street*. She said she thought it was the best Stones record. I agreed. It wasn't like you needed to be completely smitten to have a threesome, but there was this bizzaro world where I could have pictured myself being happy with a woman like Cecilia, in fact, after we were back at the tent, my head DJ played the Simon and Garfunkel song on repeat, and anyway, being comfortable with Cecilia helped ease the awkwardness of what would be our first threesome, for all of us.

"It was a mostly positive experience, once we got back to my place, we did some molly Rebecca and I had been saving for a rainy day. Then, we bared down to skin and made shapes out of our bodies, triangles and circles and spirals, we used them like machines, pumping in and out like a piston engine, rotating like a cement mixer, we suffocated each other in the steam of our sweat and we flooded ourselves in fluid exchange, the molly making the whole act sparkle like metallic paint. We laughed and laughed when we were done, watched the sunrise while drinking box wine out of our fridge, and then when the molly wore off, Cecelia went home. It was just a pleasant way to spend an evening, nothing more, nothing less. Rebecca and I decided we wanted to try it again.

"We hung out with Cecelia a few more times, and it was fun like that every time. But then Rebecca said we should start looking for other people who might be interested, that I might grow too fond of Cecelia. And like I was okay with what she was saying, I liked Cecelia, but I liked Rebecca more, and I was into the idea of trying new things, of meeting new people, of seeing the part of their world that only happened behind the curtains."

Doug sat down at the picnic table on the back patio of Griffs with a Sierra Nevada. He said, "Where'd you find this place?"

In my dreams, Robert thought to himself. He said, "Just driving down the street one day. I don't know. My grandmother was Irish. Thought it had charm." Robert looked around at the untreated wood on the side of the building, at the beer advertisements, at the clovers and Irish flags strung above their heads, from the tops of the gigantic tents out back.

"Well, it's got better charm than it does a beer selection. I'll give you that." Doug said. Robert knew it wasn't Doug's kind of a place. Part of the reason he invited him there.

"Sorry, you could have picked the place." Robert said. He lit a cigarette.

"When did you start smoking?"

None of your business, Robert thought. He said, "Did you see the menu? Want to share some wings?"

Doug took a swig of his beer. Picked up a menu that was wedged between the napkin dispenser and a salt and pepper shaker. He looked at Robert in his tank top and shorts. Then he looked down at his own designer shirt and tie. He asked, "Is that all they have? Wings?"

"No, they've got all sorts of stuff—burgers, pizza, salads. The wings are just the best is all. They make them with sauces from a local vendor. Company's run by a metal head couple. He's in a rather popular local band, Venomous Maximus, you ever heard of them?"

Doug just looked at his old friend as if he were joking.

Robert said, "Of course you haven't. I hadn't either until I started hanging out here. Anyway, if we're gonna do wings, I like the Assburn sauce the best."

Doug looked over the menu. "I might just do a Caesar salad."

"Suit yourself. But you're missing out" Robert said. Then he called out to one of the bartenders who was wiping down tables outside. "Hey, Timmy, will you bring him a Caesar salad? I'll do a ten piece order of Assburn wings, with blue cheese and fries. And I'll take another Lone Star and a Jaegermeister." He looked at Doug. "You want a shot?"

"I'd rather not." Doug said. Timmy, the bartender, departed for inside to go attend to their order. Doug looked at Robert. "So, why'd you call me out here today?"

Robert sat up in his chair. Took a drag off his cigarette. "Look, I'm just gonna come right out with it. I want out. How much do you think my half is worth?"

Doug looked concerned but not surprised. He took another sip from his beer. He said, "Well, I'd be happy to sit down with you and go over the numbers. See what we could arrange, but are you sure you want to do this? I'm happy to keep running it for a while. You can take a little more time off."

"I don't want to do that. I just want out. Make me an offer."

"Look, you and I both know I'm not going to do that without looking at the numbers first, without talking to the boys in accounting. But you remember when we started this firm? It was after I took a gap year with the law firm?"

"Yeah, I remember." Timmy, the bartender, brought back out his beer and his shot. Robert looked at Doug's half-drunk beer. He said, "You need another one? It's on me."

"Sure, I'll take another one." Timmy nodded at the two men and departed for the bar. Doug continued, "So here's what I learned taking my gap year. That I wanted to be in charge of my own destiny. I was tired of helping other companies get around the tax code. I wanted to be running something of my own. Something where I could use my legal expertise to make some real money. Because there was a cap to what I could bill at the firm. I thought it all out on that container ship I took to Africa. I was one of only three passengers. There was a lot of time to think. You know, I realized I was tired of the grind of legal life. And while real estate isn't perfect, I've been way happier since I made the switch. Hell, maybe at the end of your gap, you'll feel like real estate isn't for you, maybe you'll find yourself wanting something new, something exciting, but take a year, think it through, I'll still pay you a salary, like I got paid on my gap year. It's only fair. Anyway, why don't you join me at church this Sunday? We'll pray about it together. I'll support you no matter what you choose."

Timmy came back with the beer, the wings and the salad. A group of what appeared to be bikers came outside. One who was wearing sunglasses looked at Robert's and Doug's table and said, "You're back. Good to see you."

Robert said, "Hey man. You on your bike today? Not stuck in the cage like last time?"

"Yup, back on the bike. Got it out of the shop."

The bikers proceeded to a table in the corner. Robert took a big bite out of his first wing and fanned his tongue while chewing with his mouth open. He mumbled, "Shit, that's hot."

Doug tensed up, dumped pepper on his salad. Robert wondered what he thought about the bikers. Doug swallowed a bite he had yet to take. He said, "So, does that sound fair?"

Robert, still talking with his mouth full, said, "Look, I don't want a gap year. I just want out. I need change, and I need it now. Just make me an offer. It can be low."

"After a while, Rebecca got pretty good at asking other women to have threesomes with us, and then it was just like another item on the menu in our sex life. We found that even those who turned us down were often flattered by the request. At first, it ran counter to my idea of how American culture responded to sex, but like after I really thought about it, how much porno we watch as a country, only makes sense that so many people are walking around with desires for group sex, we just aren't talking about it. It's weird, you know, why are we wired this way, to be ashamed of the things we most want?"

"Well, that part seems almost certainly more nurture than nature. The ancients were more sexually open than we are. But the nature part is that we all desire a pretty wide ranging set of flavors compared to what we ever actually sample, and shame might just be a response to allow for social foundation, so that we don't put our freedom over another's, but you're right that we likely take it too far. I can't give away any specifics, client privilege and all, but you're not the first person who's sat on that couch and brought up a desire for group sex. You're not even the second or third. So, yeah, it's way more common than we think."

"We found that people liked to talk about it, liked having the permission. When you were at the bar having a few drinks and just up front and honest about wanting a no strings attached evening of fun, generally speaking, they responded favorably, whether the answer was yes or no. The noes often prompted even more conversation about it than the yeses (maybe because they didn't want to fully talk themselves out of it). But once curiosities were piqued, we would all rethink those boring traditional views about monogamy. Or at least, that was how I was thinking about it at the time. There were advantages to monogamy I hadn't considered, but I still believe we should have a looser enforcement of monogamy. Like adultery, so long as it isn't serially insensitive, probably shouldn't be comparable to theft and murder the way Christian commandments would lead us to believe, it certainly shouldn't be the immediate end to any relationship when it happens. Sometimes people just want to try something different for a night. If we could be more open about that fact, I think a lot of relationships would be better off.

"Anyway, Rebecca and I got plenty of yeses to our advances. Soon, it seemed like we weren't even having sex just the two of us anymore. But again, I'm not trying to brag about our prolificness, just trying to tap into this idea I keep having about how physical experience constructs mental experience, and how the physical longing of our bodies for each other is the same basic feeling of longing we use to build the picture of ourselves, how we choose who we are by which desires we choose to follow, and that because we choose who we are, we create the story of ourselves. But it gets deeper than that even, because of the way our thoughts come to us as received instead of built, we often also have to make a God, a structure to inform what we desire most, to be a fundamental part of the life process instead of just a particular life, so we make a God, but really God is just a symbol of our inability to be filled, God can be anything, it's just whatever you insert into that longing to make the sinking feeling go away, which also never makes it go away. Sex is the only thing, to me, where it's different, where it doesn't feel like substitution but like you actually get what you want. The longing only comes back after you're done, but in the moment, sex works. You feel alive."

"So I guess God can't be sex in your metaphysics? God is the search for something like sex that isn't sex, like God has to be something that can be preserved."

"I think he or she (or whatever God is) could be sex too. I

mean, I don't really believe in God, but I just mean, wherever sex fits into that hierarchy, with drugs and working and relationships and money and everything else we fill our lives with, sex actually makes me feel whole, even if only temporarily, if a force like that were eternal in its human particularity, you'd certainly feel like a God."

"Maybe that means sex is just your God, then?"

"I'm not like a sex addict or anything, at least, I don't think. We were active and experimental, but we weren't like negatively impacted if we struck out a few times in a row either. I'm not trying to make it seem like it was everything. Just that it was the best thing. That no matter how much society seems to want us to search for these long term fulfilling goals, which again, there are certain advantages to, to the way they control longing, but besides all that, pleasure is still more powerful a motivator because pleasure is self-actualization, and sexual pleasure seems to be the purest form of pleasure. And anyway, we were maybe more radical in our sex life than the average couple, but in the world of swingers and polyamorous lifestyle folks, we were still probably considered squares, wannabes."

"No, I think I get what you're saying. So anyway, you were going to tell me how Titus figured into all this, with you and Rebecca?"

"So, she asks me one day if we can try having a threesome with a man. If I'd be okay with that? And truthfully, I had mixed feelings. But I told her I'd be okay with it, regardless, because I wanted to be fair, since we'd already had several women. Then, she asked me to find someone.

"But like I didn't have that same openness, that honesty of feeling, that willingness to expose and explain my desire to other men that Rebecca had with women. So I asked Titus, because I trusted him."

"You trusted him? That guy?"

"Well, look, he was my best friend, as hard as that is for you to believe, but there was one other reason too. I was pretty sure he'd be down for it. Like I don't know why it's so hard for me to talk about it, I don't think there's anything wrong with men having sex with each other, or with men being attracted to each other, but then again, I have this instinctual discomfort with my own exploits being known, with my own desires being found out. You see, I subscribe to the theory that we're all a little bisexual, no matter how we eventually identify ourselves. So like Titus and I, well, we used to experiment together when we were kids."

"Wait, are you saying you were worried about being thought of as gay because of what you did as a kid?"

"No. I mean, I don't know."

"You do realize that when boys start puberty, it's common for them to play with each other like that. It's quite natural. It's just about discovering your body, and you start doing that with whoever's body is more like yours."

"Yeah, I think I've heard that before. But with Titus and I it went on and off and on again for a lot longer than just pre-adolescence, or even adolescence for that matter, but it was also never anything more than purely physical expression. I never felt anything romantically about it. But yeah, I think the last time we slept together was in our early twenties. We did eventually stop, I think because of me, I just grew gradually more and more uncomfortable with it, and then I eventually met my first long term girlfriend, and I came to realize that I really just preferred women. I mean, I didn't totally rule out the idea of a man in the future, I just wouldn't be seeking out that type of relationship anymore, and consequently, Titus and I didn't have that type of relationship anymore. But we never actually talked about any of what happened, even while we were doing it, we never talked about it, and we certainly didn't after it stopped.

"So when I say I trusted him, it was that I knew he wouldn't say anything later, and I knew he knew what I liked, should we venture into that during the threesome. Anyway, he did say yes when I asked him. It was at a hotel party the three of us had gone to in Galveston. I had asked Rebecca what she thought about the idea of Titus, and she said she thought I should be asking myself that question, but because I couldn't think of any other men who I'd be comfortable enough to bring it up around, I said I was fine with it. Then, we're at this party, at one of those cheap places with the wood panel walls and the vibrating beds and all that. The rest of the party took off to the beach, just the three of us were left inside, we'd had quite a bit to drink, and while Rebecca was in the bathroom, I laid it on the table for Titus.

Titus smiled, he grabbed my cock through my pants. He said, "My little Ganymede has come back to me."

"I hated it when he called me that. Like why couldn't I have been the God in that relationship, even if he admittedly was the more dom of the two of us, especially in the bedroom. Anyway, when Rebecca came out of the bathroom, we all agreed we probably had enough time before everyone got back. But then, I don't know, something about the way Titus smiled at her once we were all naked, something about the way he looked like he wanted to devour me, like I kept second guessing what I was doing. Somewhere along the line, when they'd started kissing and rubbing on each other, I just put my clothes on, left the room."

Robert held back the orange-brown curtains at the Palace Inn on 45 and Telephone. It was a pay-by-the-hour joint with a blue-and-white sign out front that flickered not from intended effect but from faulty wiring. The handrails were rusted, the bricks were cracked, and the landscaping even when properly maintained seemed to give the place an artificial and perverse idea of hospitality that was essential to the clientele it attracted for business. Robert stared through the cracked window like he was searching for an apparition. Each wheeze of the old window unit blew out a moldy stench along with the not-quite-cool-enough air he could feel humidifying his kneecaps under his khaki shorts. He'd been expecting Gregor to come back, and every noise outside brought him back to the window again to look out on no one walking up just yet—all he could see now was a multiplicity of reflections of his face, broken pieces of those faces, and broken pieces of those pieces, all directing a fractal gaze back at him. It was like a second mirror stage, minus the mirror, a marker for the onset of the infancy of middle age.

His phone dinged on the table across the room, which was only about four or five steps away. He left the window. Went to retrieve it. It had to be Gregor. He picked up his phone. Saw on the home screen: where are u

He didn't reply.

It dinged again: Cora is crying

He wouldn't answer, not now.

Another ding, this time no words. Just an angry face emoji.

It was his wife. What was she, fifteen years old, he thought to himself? True, he was missing his youngest daughter's birthday party, but she was only eight, she'd have plenty more of them. Plus, when she saw her present, she was going to freak out. He'd gotten her a Mac Book, partly for him too, so that she could keep herself entertained.

He'd meant to go to the party, but Gregor, who went by BEETLEG364 online, on the deep web, finally sent him a return message, weeks later, telling him Griff's was no good, that he wanted someplace more private, that he had the JD, and it had to be now, but then again, when Robert gave him the money, he changed his tune, said he still had to go pick it up from a friend. Of course, if Robert was ever going to get back to being the father he could be, the father he wanted to be, the father he used to be, or the one he already was, however it worked, then he would have to figure out how to get rid of Stevie, or to figure out who Stevie was, and why he was in his head messing up all his relationships. The JD had to be the only answer. The hospital hadn't worked, the therapist Betty had demanded he go to, Dr. Thiery, while perhaps a good listener he had to admit, ultimately, didn't do much for him either. He was either going to find the JD, or it would all be lost. He hoped Gregor would come through. The other Beetle, Titus' Beetle, would have found it.

Robert walked over to the bed and sat down. There was a merchant ship painting hanging over the rotting fake-oak headboard, a rotary phone on the side table by the bed, hadn't seen one of those since, well, since that hotel room, which was pretty close in decor to this room—where Titus, Rebecca, and he had...

But he didn't want to think about that right now. He just wanted Gregor to show up. He ran his hand along the gritty, slightly sticky aqua-colored comforter before moving his hand over to the single drawer on the side table. He opened it. A Gideon's Bible. He flipped it to the Book of Job. One of the few things both Robert and Stevie had in common, their affinity for Job, even if they had different reasons for admiring the man, *historically* speaking (if he could call it that). He tried to read Job to pass the time, but impatience buzzed in his head like an alarm clock, if only he could have pulled out the internal clock in his head like how the one in the room had been yanked out of the wall. What had it been now, two hours? Was Gregor ripping him off?

He didn't so much care about the money. There was plenty more where that came from, at least, there still should be. He'd pay Gregor again if he needed to. He only wished he could check in with him, but Gregor had demanded he not send him any messages that weren't encrypted, and he didn't have his laptop with him. He could wait a little longer, though, in case anything had been held up.

He shut the book when he realized he wouldn't hear it over the sounds of the other voices in his head. He put it back in the drawer, stood up, and began pacing around the room, opening the closet, peering in at the empty set of hangers, at the ironing board. He closed the closet door and walked over to the sink in the bathroom, running the water and turning it off again. There was a coffee maker on the counter covered in plastic wrap, a symbol of sanitation, just below where a roach was crawling across the wall. It wasn't the type of place he would have brought his family to, but Stevie wasn't entirely unfamiliar with places like this, so Robert felt a little more at home than he should have, despite the anxiety over the JD.

A heavy-handed knock at the door. He walked back over toward the window. Gregor was back, he thought, before looking out and realizing it wasn't Gregor. A gaunt man stood there who he'd never met before, wearing canary yellow sweatpants, white athletic socks with flip-flops, and a hot pink tank top. He had Blue Blockers hanging from his neckline and was chewing on a toothpick. He knocked again. "I can see you in there. Open up man."

Robert opened the door.

"What's up? You holding in here motherfucker?"

The man was white, and Robert didn't want to feel racist for assuming how he should sound, but he did find it interesting that the further he delved into the drug scene, the more he found all these white dudes who talked just like Samuel L. Jackson (as written by Quentin Tarantino). Like how even in their own addictions, they associated drug use with criminality and criminality with blackness, like an outer display to distance themselves from their own inner addicts—or maybe it was the opposite, that they were distancing themselves from their own whiteness, from the power associated with privilege, which carried all sorts of responsibilities they were afraid they could never live up to. Robert couldn't judge them, not completely. Seemed like he was destined to become one of them, he could feel it, maybe he already was, even if he hadn't yet adopted the dialect.

"I asked you a question, you gonna answer me? You holding homey?"

"Holding what?"

"Holding what? Crack, fool, I got cash, I wanna get high. Sheeeit, holding what? What you think I was talking bout, yo dick?" He walked inside without asking. Sat in the chair by the table.

"Oh, sorry. No, no crack in here. But maybe we could help each other out. I'm looking for JD. You know where to find any?" Robert pulled out his wallet.

"Some what? JD? What the fuck is that?" The man threw his shades down on the table. Took the toothpick out of his mouth and twirled it between his fingers, put his feet up on the bed, with his filthy shoes still on them.

"Plant extract. From the *Lupinus deum*. You smoke it." Robert remained standing. Not sure whether he should join him at the table.

"From the whatty what? Is that English? Fucking white people man, y'all will smoke whatever the fuck." The white man finished his sentence with a hearty laugh. He didn't appear to be speaking ironically.

Robert said, "Sorry. It's a hallucinogen. This guy Gregor said he'd get it for me. You know him? He suggested this place as a meet up."

"Don't know no Gregor either. Say, you got a car? If you want to get high, I know a spot down the way. Sell us some shit get us so high, you'll forget JD even existed. Just got to drive me over there."

"Robert! Wake up. Wake the fuck up right now." He rolled over into the couch. "Robert!" He was being pummeled with something soft, a pillow. "Robert! Get up! You want to tell me why our mortgage payment bounced?"

He sat up. He saw his wife standing over him. He said,

"Hmmm. That's funny."

"Funny? No, Robert, it's not funny. Did Doug not pay you? What's going on?"

"I sold Doug my half. He doesn't owe me anything."

"What? When?"

"I don't know. A while ago. Last year some time."

"Last year? So where the fuck have you been going every-day? What'd you do with the money?"

He just stared at her. How did he explain a budding drug problem and some really bad Bitcoin investments? To his credit, he at least felt a little guilty, which wasn't always the case when he was fighting with Betty. Like no matter how much he didn't like Robert's wife—or his own wife, whoever she was, he was tired of the guesswork—but she didn't deserve this. He'd fucked up royally, no matter whose life he was fucking with. He started to cry.

"Oh Jesus. No, stop that. You don't get to make me feel bad right now. Do you still have any money left?"

He let the tears answer.

"So, we're fucking broke? What do you expect me to do? What are you going to do? Are you still seeing Dr. Thiery?"

He let the tears answer again.

"No, of course you're not. It's over. I called an attorney this morning, paperwork should already be in the mail. I'm just hoping the bank will work with me on the house." She walked over and kissed him with malevolence. "Do you think you can be gone by the time the girls get home from school? I don't want them to see you like this."

He looked down at himself. His shirt was covered in some sort of mysterious black stains. He had been sleeping in his shoes, which had mud caked around them.

"And clean up this couch. What the fuck?"

He stood up. Something fell from his lap and hit the carpet. Betty walked over and picked it up. He doubted she'd ever seen one in person before, but she seemed to know what it was.

"You're smoking crack? Is that what you're doing? Jesus, do you remember lecturing me about smoking pot in college?"

He finally said, "I'm sorry."

He even said it in a way that sounded like he meant it for once. Betty walked over and gave him a hug. The fire from her rage was all burnt up, and now she was just staring at a pathetic wreck of a man who was once her husband. He kept crying.

"Get some help Robert. I'm not going to sit here and console you all day. Be gone by the time I get home with our daughters, and stay away until you're ready to be a father. This is goodbye."

She got up, walked over to the dining room table, gathered her purse, and walked out the back door, leaving Robert with nothing but a cruel reflection of himself inside a cruel reflection on himself.

Bob walked out of the invisibly clear glass doors of the parish center at St. Paul's United Methodist Church. The weekly Saturday night meeting of the H.O.W. Group of Alcoholics Anonymous had just concluded. A congregation formed outside the house of worship in the freshly tarred parking lot—the smell matched Bob's mood perfectly.

Lighter flicks clicked through the air like S.O.S. signals. There was a unified hum of all the stories the people who had been inside were now exchanging on the outside based on those stories they'd just heard on the inside. Bob walked off by himself, took a sip of weak watery coffee before setting his steaming paper cup on the hood of some stranger's car. He lit a cigarette and thought to himself, now what?

He figured he might as well call his sponsor, who he had to call once a day. He picked up the cup, took another sip of coffee, set it back down, and scrolled through his phone. He saw the contact, Jersey Dade, JD as they called him in the rooms, Bob thought it was a sign when he had first asked him ninety days ago, "Do you, um, maybe want to, um, take me through the steps?"

It felt like the first time he asked a girl to "go with him." JD hadn't agreed that night, only gave Bob his phone number, said "Call me anytime you need to, day or night, we'll talk about the steps later." Then he grabbed Bob in a bear hug and said, "Hey man. Be cool. It's gonna be okay."

Now, JD wasn't so nice anymore. Bob reached into his pocket, pulled a purple chip from it, heard JD's voice in his head before he even called him. "You got that fourth step for me man?"

Sure enough, it was exactly how JD answered the phone. Bob said, "I got ninety days."

"Ninety days won't keep you sober like the steps will." He could imagine JD on the other end, doing that thing he did where he put his elbow on his dining room table and bounced his hand up and down, palm side up, to the rhythm of his admonishments.

"I'm working on it. I'm just trying to get it right. I worked on it a little yesterday. It's just taking more time than I thought it would." Bob lied, threw his smoke to the ground and put it out with his shoe, feeling the paper around the filter rip underneath.

"This disease don't take no time off. You ever just look for crack for a little bit, until you could figure out how to smoke it right? If you ain't finished with the fourth step, you should be writing it instead of calling me."

"You said to call every day."

"Look dude, quit making excuses, and quit thinking about it. Just write that shit down. Like it says in the book. Make four columns. Who am I resentful at? Why? What was their part? And what was my part? Then just write the answers in, short, don't need to describe the whole scene. Just plain and simple. The idea is not to think. You see, I got me a thinking disease, and if you like me, you got yo self a thinking disease too, you feel me? So don't think. Write. That thinking shit gonna land you right back outside that motherfucking door."

Bob thought back to Christian, the guy he'd met in the Palace Inn, what, must have been two, three, shit, almost four years ago now by this point, but the guy who gave him his first taste, his first running buddy. JD sounded just like him. It was uncanny. Another white Samuel L. Jackson. Bob had caught himself talking like that several times too, rolling down Gillette street in Freedman's Town, saying out the window, "Looking for a twinkie. Looking for a twinkie. Who's holdin'?"

Bob thought back to how he'd learned to score, how you could tell who the dealers were by the inconspicuously conspicuous walk they all adopted, up and down the block, slow with a limp. Then again, in Freedman's Town, where he did most of his "shopping," once the first black subdivision in Houston marked by a historical landmark by the entrance to the neighborhood, the whole community it seemed had turned into a crack den, hardly anyone who lived there wasn't involved in the drug trade, or at least, that's how it felt, like any neighborhood, there were likely all sorts of nameless faceless residents who wanted nothing to do with it, people whose rage at his presence there could simply be ignored on account of his own myopia. But Bob had learned the game between the dealers and fiends, and the game had taken him to a place where he could almost now claim a third identity inside his already crowded head—Bob L., the recovering crackhead.

"Hello? You still there?" JD sounded irritated, like he always did. Bob hadn't thought this was how sponsors were supposed to treat people, but all the other newcomers he knew, Terry D. and Shelly R. and Leif H., they all had similar complaints. It was either accept tough love or no love at all.

Bob said, "Yeah, I'm here."

"So, what are you going to do?"

The crowd in the parking lot was now breaking into mini-crowds, the sober alcoholics and addicts making late night plans for dinner and coffee. He wanted to go out, to celebrate his ninety days of continuous sobriety, but he knew JD would accept no answers other than agreeing to work on his personal inventory, to get it finished tonight, so that he could take the fifth step, which was essentially the same thing as a Christian reconciliation. The idea of purging, of penance, of a confession of your worst of sins. JD stressed how it would be the first real feeling of relief he'd find, the first act of faith, of giving yourself over to the spiritual journey, of aligning yourself with the program inside of the program. JD told Bob that anyone could do steps one through three, which was only admitting the problem and that you weren't the solution. The real work came in accepting the help, which was in the book, requiring book work. JD also liked to remind him that he would've done some homework for a free rock without thinking twice about it during his using career.

Bob said what he wanted JD to hear tonight. "I'll work on it when I get home from the meeting."

"Don't bullshit me. Remember when I asked if you was willing to do whatever it takes?"

"Yeah, yeah."

"Don't yeah yeah me neither. This shit is serious. You got a disease that's gonna kill you motherfucker. You gotta want this shit. You gotta be willing. Ya dig?"

"I want my wife and kids back, that's for sure." Probably a mistake to say that, but he couldn't help thinking about Betty. It had been a year since they'd last spoken. He was holding out a pessimistic hope (it was the best he could do to sustain himself at this point) that maybe his effort would mean something to her. He wished he'd have realized how much he would have missed her after she'd been gone, after he found out she shacked up with Doug, after Doug had also left his wife (in less dramatic fashion), Bob had come to realize the mistake he'd made. It was then that he decided to get help and then it took a little while longer to actually do it.

JD sounded angrier than before. "Say what? You telling me you got that back disease? Sheeit, you ain't gonna make it another week with that attitude."

Bob said, "No. I want this for me too. Just like if it would help with her is all. Wait, what do you mean by back disease?"

"Back disease, motherfucker. I want my wife back, want my kids back, want my house back, want my bottle back, want my crackpipe back. This ain't no get yo shit back program. This a learn to humble yo self just enough to find your higher power program, so you can find what little satisfaction you can with whatever your present circumstances might be, you hear me?"

He did and didn't hear him. Like sure, striving to be happy could include a life without his ex-wife, theoretically. But he wasn't sure how to get over the guilt of it all, and he had this feeling of longing for her that he hadn't experienced since they were a young couple. He figured it was good, if he could just get her back, if he could only prove he was worthy to start over with, if he could get her away from Doug.

Comparing Betty to Rebecca certainly hadn't been fair. It was the biggest mistake he'd made, he now realized. What woman could live up to a fantasy? Because it was a fantasy, he knew that. He came to realize that Stevie must have been this character he invented to deal with his own midlife crisis, to deal with his own sense of inadequacy, his inability to be happy even after getting all the stuff he'd always been promised would make him happy. His story was typical in that way. He came to realize the structure of it was typical, even if some of the details were unique. He told JD, "I don't know, my story isn't the saddest in the world, but it is complicated."

JD responded so fast it was like he was talking over him. "You think you terminally unique or something? Hell, man, you know I used to suck dick for rocks? Thought I was the only motherfucker who ever sank so low. Thought I wasn't worth nothing in the world. Come in here, find out a bunch of motherfuckers sucked a lot of dicks for a whole lot of drugs. Why not just fess up? Tell me what it is you think is so bad. That blast was worth it, wasn't it? That shit used to make my balls tickle when I'd exhale. I'd do anything to get more. Shit, man, I used to live in a refrigerator box behind the Circle K on White Oak, thinking I was hot shit too, cause the guy that slept next to me by the dumpster only had a sleeping bag. So try telling me some shit I ain't never heard before. I dare you to motherfucker."

Robert looked at people getting into their cars, ready to depart. He needed to get off the phone if he wanted to catch coffee with someone. He said. "It's really not that big of a deal. I'm gonna go work on my steps now."

"You do that. And when you call me tomorrow, it better be cause you're ready for me to hear your fifth step."

Bob took a sip from a quite delicious and quite strong *granita* as he left the counter. He felt his pupils dilate. The drinks were better on the sober side of the aisle, at least, they were when you got away from the meeting rooms. He looked up into the balcony to see if his friends had secured the couch. John S. and Susan T. were the first to arrive. Fuck, he muttered under his breath as he made his way up the narrow staircase.

They weren't his favorite members of his sober clique, which wasn't his favorite clique to begin with. John smelled like a litter box. He didn't so much own cats as he just let strays in from off the street, running an unlicensed temporary animal shelter from his duplex apartment. He always complained about the neighbors complaining about him feeding the animals. He'd say things like, "I'd feed the neighbors too if they were hard up. It's just what one spiritual being

142

is supposed to do for another." He'd actually refer to himself that way, as a spiritual being. Bob suspected he didn't even have that much of drug problem, he claimed his drug of choice was weed, like who gets that addicted to weed, the guy was probably just lonely, and the program was a catch-all for all sorts of society's dregs.

Susan always talked about the decor, every time they came here, to the Agora Cafe on Westheimer, which was at least once a week, oftentimes twice, as the daily schedule of meeting, coffee, home, meeting, coffee, home, meeting, coffee, home, only allowed for so much variation. She'd say, "Oh, this place reminds me of one of those little cafes we used to visit in Athens, overlooking the ruins." Or she'd say, "Those busts are so adorable. They add so much character to this place." Word on her was her husband had been a famous DJ in the rave scene, that they did an annual festival in Athens called Scream Antiquity, in fact, they toured tent festivals across Europe for a decade, developing profound meth and ecstasy habits. Susan moved back to the states to live with her mother after the husband committed suicide in London. She'd been sober for five years now, but her short term memory had yet to recover at the same rate of speed as her body had appeared to.

Bob sat down next them on the couch. Susan said, "This place makes me want to visit the Parthenon again." John just laughed, stuffed his hands into his armpits. Bob might catch him smelling his fingers later. Tim G. walked up the stairs shortly after Bob, eating a pastry along with his coffee. He spoke with his mouth full, spitting out crumbs as he sat down, "You guys tried this new twist thing they got?"

Bob thought about how, food or not, he was tired of twists, and what they might have in store. He said to Tim, "Heard you got six months a couple days ago. Congrats man. That's a long time. I'm at four and a half now."

"Well congrats to you. This is the longest I've gotten in here since '03, after my first wife died."

None of their stories seemed to end well, even when they stayed sober, which wasn't that often, it didn't seem. Susan said, "Anyone seen Kurt M. lately?"

Tim said, "Shit, you haven't heard? He went out last week, OD'd, still alive but he had a stroke, lots of brain damage. He'll need someone to take care of him for the rest of his life." Tim put his hands together in a gesture of prayer, looked up at the ceiling, and said, "There but for the grace of God go I."

Jeff said, "I heard that. Some of us got to go back out so that the rest of us know where it's nice and cozy." Easy for the guy with the weed habit to say, thought Bob.

Mindy walked up the stairs. It was the whole reason Bob had agreed to come to coffee tonight, knowing she'd be coming. JD had put the idea in his head when they were still sponsor and sponsee, before JD had ditched him. JD told Bob that normally he didn't recommend sponsees get involved in relationships in their first year of sobriety, but he also knew Bob needed to do something to get his mind off of Betty. Said he caught Mindy eying Bob at one of the meetings. JD told him, "Man, Betty, she got yo head so messed up, like you just need to remember what other pussy smells like, you feel me? Don't fall in love, though. We don't be needing that problem neither."

Mindy sat down next to him. She said, "Hi. You're JD's sponsee. How's it going?"

"Well, I was his sponsee."

"What happened?"

"The fourth step happened."

"Oh sweetie. Sorry to hear that. You know, sometimes having trouble with getting through the steps is just a personality issue. You'll find another sponsor." He didn't tell her he wasn't looking. She continued, "And no need to worry about the fourth step. It's like Nike, Just do it."

Bob thought how "Just do it" was a rather odd piece of

wisdom to give to a drug addict. He looked at Mindy. There was nothing special about her. She was nice, but he didn't feel anything. He'd heard the name outside the meeting and thought back to that conversation with JD. There was nothing else. He shouldn't have come. Even if he had been genuinely attracted to her, he wouldn't have known what to say to her to strike up a conversation—hi, I'm Bob, and when I'm not being disinvited from my own daughter's high school graduation, I'm being asked to sign a document for my younger daughter that gives up my parental rights, if you play your cards right, you might just get to walk home with this prize.

He still wanted Betty, even when her tone was short, like it had been on the phone yesterday, the first time he'd heard from her in ages. "Robert," she still called him that, "Anne told me she invited you to her graduation, but I really think you should stay away. It's her day. You can find another time to reunite. Take her to lunch or something. As for Cora, well, you'll find out anyway, but Doug and I are getting married, and I want you to sign your rights over to him. The state will let you off the hook for all that child support."

He'd agreed to all of it. Figured he didn't have any choice at this point. Hearing her voice had been good, though, no matter how negative the content of the conversation was, no matter how much dimmer it made that pessimistic light of hope he still ever so slightly clung to.

Mindy asked, "Are you okay? You look down."

Bob said, "I'm fine."

"Fucked up, insecure, neurotic, and emotional?"

It was a joke they'd told in the rooms. Not the first time he'd heard it. Funny only cause it was true. An addict never wasn't those things. He certainly never wasn't. But all the endless conversations that went exactly the same way were wearing on him, and Bob was desperately in need of a connection that wasn't superficial. Mindy wouldn't turn out to be that. He still laughed at her joke, to be nice.

He said, "Guilty as charged."

She gave him her number. She said, "If you ever need to talk." He wondered if JD had put any ideas in her head too. Usually, only men approached men and women approached women, or at least, that was how it was supposed to go down among the more respectful members, of which there weren't many. In fact, JD telling him to get laid was part of the reason Bob didn't finish his fourth step—or, maybe it wasn't part of the reason, but it was part of what made him glad he didn't. The other part of the program that he couldn't stand, aside from the sheer boredom, was how many predatory sexual practices were left unspoken, how many old men preyed on newcomers, how many sponsors served as pickup artists for their sponsees. He didn't want any part of that. He told Mindy thanks in a way that would make her realize he didn't completely mean it.

The lights went down, the house music started to play, releasing him from the need to feel like he had to talk to her simply because some storyline had been introduced by some authority figure in his life. The music was some sort of electronic music with a Mediterranean flare. He forgot it was Wednesday. Belly dancing night at Agora. He would have avoided coming if he'd remembered, even with hearing Mindy's name mentioned as being a member of the party.

He heard a tambourine coming up the stairs, a belly dancer soon appeared at the doorway. Ribbons hung from her clothes, spinning in rhythm to her movements. He heard some frat boy at a table behind him say, "Bro, isn't this the best? Man, what I'd do to her."

Like they didn't even care about the artistic aspect of it, the power of the dancer, the magic she held over the viewer. They might as well have been in a strip club. In fact, the whole scene was too much like a strip club, he thought, as he looked around the room at the crowd that was a little too businessman heavy. He told his friends he was going to the bathroom, and then he walked out the back door and shuffled the half-mile back to his apartment. When he locked the door behind him, he thought, one more day in the books.

Bob walked on autopilot, turned the corner from W. Gray onto Gillette. It was like his ego was above his head watching his id make all the movements without any consideration of his intentions. He yelled at himself, internally, Don't do it! But he knew better than anyone it was too late. His first thought was quickly followed by a, Well, maybe just a little taste.

But not on today of all days, he told himself. The day that Doug and Betty, somewhere across town were tying the knot, the final erasure of his old identity. He had wanted a new life for himself, one he could be happy with on his own terms and not just hers, but he couldn't take it. He looked at the row houses and saw a group of boys, none of them could have been older than sixteen, he motioned toward one with his hand, a hand he had a hundred dollar bill curled up inside, already knowing a hundred dollars wouldn't cut it. He'd be back later today.

The kid took his money, motioned him to go around the side of the house. Another kid was waiting, handed him what he wanted. Bob stuffed the rocks into his mouth, maneuvering them underneath his lips, in case he got stopped on his way out of the neighborhood, where the police sometimes posted up on the corner.

He shuffled his feet back toward the pay-by-the-week hotel that doubled as his apartment, his mind now telling him to flush it when he got home. Then he stopped at the convenience store on Dunlavy, to pick up a stem. Outside of the store, there was some crazy old preacher shouting verses from Revelation at people passing by. He handed Bob a religious tract. Bob stuffed it into his back pocket.

He walked into the store and bought one of those kits with the glass rose and the Chore Boy. The cashier and Bob exchanged a knowing stare that was probably equally uncomfortable for both men. Bob walked out of the store and back up the broken sidewalk, pointed like a compass, straight toward his destination. Now that he had a bullet and a gun, there wasn't much use in trying to talk himself out of committing the crime. His neural network stopped running the sobriety program and returned to its regularly scheduled feature, Extreme Makeover: Homeless Edition. The grand reveal was that his father never loved him and his mother loved him too much (if you're still searching for motivations when the bus drives off).

He sat on the mattress inside his room, alone, completely. No friends or family anywhere. He stared at the drab yellow carpet, at the holes in the Sheetrock. He had a lighter in one hand and the only salvation he could make sense of anymore in the other. When the smoke started billowing, he sucked and sucked and sucked and didn't stop until the glass dick in his hand forced him to come. Then he laid back on the bed and let the tinnitus lilt him toward a permanent slumber while the goosebumps on his arms marched forward like killer ants. His legs piked violently, against his will, then he fell back to the bed, his hands went limp, the pipe fell to the mattress, melting a hole in the musty sheets. His last earthly feeling was a surge from his left shoulder down to his big toe, his heart in full-on nuclear explosion mode. The war was finally over, post-apocalypse became him.

He crossed over. He was still turned on somehow, in a different body, not the same kind of body, walking into a tunnel that felt like a birth canal. Then, it was as if he were flying through a jet stream, wondering if the enemy would strike again, wondering if he were headed toward the place they called heaven. He heard a screech and saw his engines explode in a burst of Technicolor light. Then everything was dark, like he was in a vacuum.

He heard what sounded like a projector fire up, and all of a sudden he was inside of a constellation, in a hyperspace limbo. There were colored lights everywhere, like on a Lite Brite, in the forms of trees and flowers and grass and birds and bees and butterflies, all swaying to what couldn't have been a breeze. It must have been a hologram, he thought, there was no wind here—in the Void.

It came to him as if in a memory, not Robert's nor Stevie's nor Bob's, but just a memory from memory itself, more like from the Memory, the very process of memory, he was in the place where souls go to become reborn. It was a personal Judgment Day, or a Post-Judgment Day.

There was movement in one of the trees and he looked over. Titus was hanging from his knees from one of the branches. He was carrying a lighting bolt, like Zeus. He said, "Welcome to your Destiny, my Ganymede."

When he looked back up, he was surrounded by what he assumed must have been other gods and goddesses, or angels, or whatever. They also had luminous bodies and all appeared to be sex fluid, in that they were morphing between having women's and men's genitalia, like they were hermaphroditic but not in a fixed way. Titus put his cock in front of his face. He looked down at a luminous pair of breasts, realizing he—or she or they or some other ill-fitting catch-all term—was one of them. He vaguely remembered being here.

Titus said, "Come on. You dirty little whore."

He had the vague sense that he might have been Rebecca, that they had become a unity of soul, that Titus was taunting him, he wanted it, though, that was the problem, that he did, oh yes, he wanted it. While he had Titus' cock in his mouth, gagging and slurping like in the dirtiest porno movies he'd ever watched, another figure approached from behind and began to fuck him. All around him, gods and goddesses and spirits were moaning. They were splayed out in all sorts of different positions, morphing between male and female and other spectral varieties of gender he had never encountered before, not like this anyway.

149

Then he realized he was a male again, fucking some other figure, who appeared to be like a version of Shiva or something. It was too much, he thought, too much pleasure. He felt like he was going to explode. No, he didn't like this. He wanted it to stop, how did it stop? He was getting fucked again. This hyperspace orgy. He wanted no more, no more of this endless act of life creation.

But then he was a she again, and he was enjoying their-self. Yes, it felt good, so good, yes, no, wait, not good, yes good, no, yes, wait, no, yes, wait, no, oh, oh, oh, ooooh, oooooh, oooooooh, ooooooooooooooh.

Overcome with emotion, they began to cry LED tears, which felt more like they were being pulled from their face than as if they were falling. They didn't know if they were Stevie, or Rebecca, or Robert, or Bob, or whoever else might be sharing this frequency of identity formation. There were less and less figures in the orgy, but who was still there now appeared as giants. They were a giant too.

The angel who had been fucking them was now inside him, not in the cheesy sex cliché sort of way, but like actually inside him, then two become one again, but a different one. And then another one started fucking him, and they were inside her, and another one, and they were a they again, and another one, until it was only he and Titus again.

He said, "What is this?"

Titus said, "Don't you remember Olympus? Nothing to be scared of."

Then Titus grabbed her by the hair, female hair, and took him from behind, kept calling them the whore of Babylon, until they accepted that it must have been the case. Then, he looked back over his shoulder and realized Titus wasn't there, that he was the only creature in this entire universe. He was the Zeus, he was the father God, the Buddha, he was Jesus Christ, he was everything and nothing, the end all and the be all, the alpha and the omega, and he was masturbating, and he was powerful. He could feel it coming, his magnificent orgasm, he kept stroking until his load came out like a genesis, the semen dripping down, spiraling into a vortex. He called his creation The Milky Way, and he was satisfied, and it was good.

And then a beam of light shot out of the galaxy and hit him in the chest, and he was just sitting in a room again, a screen sat in front of him, flashing, Game Over, Game Over, Game Over. It was fading out. So this is death, he thought.

Stevie woke up on Titus' floor yelling, "Dying is a game. Dying is a game. Dying is a game." Despite his realization, there was no agency, he had no control over the voice or the content. The walls were breathing. Holy shit, he thought, what the fuck just happened? He looked at the clock on the wall, it was 3:30. It hadn't even been an hour, and yet, it felt like it had been years since he'd been here. How much longer did he have until this stuff wore off?

"Shut up! Shut up man! We've got to stop this, before it all implodes in on itself."

Titus was behind him. Stevie looked down at his jeans, which were wet around the crotch. Had they?

Titus was pacing, drooling from his mouth, wild-eyed. He said, "What the fuck did you do man? What the fuck did you do?"

His jaw was trembling in between rants. He was rubbing the top of his head, pulling at his hair. Stevie looked around the room, at the pentagrams, at the golden lamps. There were holes in the walls, posters were ripped at the corners, hanging in tattered threads of their former selves. He remembered Titus telling him about the apocalyptic trip spot. Maybe it wasn't just Titus' version of apocalypse, maybe every creation of an apocalypse is inherently real, and now they were inside one, which would set off other apocalypses.

Titus kept going, "We're stuck. Stuck like fucking Chuck. In a loop. Boop boop bee doop. We gotta escape. Grab your cape. Let's get out of town. We're hero bound."

Titus' rhyming was new. There was another voice in the room. Coming out of the speakers. He remembered. Alan Watts, their favorite hippie theorist. "I find that the sensation of an ego inside a bag of skin is really a hallucination."

He looked at the television. Orgy of the Dead by Ed Wood was on the screen. What a terrible film. He reached into his pocket looking for his keys, pulled out a religious tract. Wait, had his death all been a hallucination too? Or was he hallucinating now? Where had he been? And where was he really? And what was really real? When would he be okay to go home (wherever that was, wherever a where was)?

He tried to stand, but he was still too wobbly, his balance off. He fell back down and landed on his face. Titus said, "End of the line, rise and shine, buddy boy, praise be, joy to the world, you can't go anywhere when your life is unfurled."

Titus came and sat down across from Stevie on the floor. In his hands were two pistols and an egg timer. He winked before speaking again, this time minus the rhyme. "You're going to think I'm crazy. But we've got to stop it. Trust me. There's no time to discuss. When this goes off, so do these pistols."

He twisted the timer, set it on the floor between them. Passed a pistol to Stevie, and kept one for himself. Stevie looked down at the revolver in his hand, unsure what to do. Titus modeled. He pointed the other gun at Stevie's forehead, said, "Now you do the same. It's gotta be exact."

Stevie pointed back. He heard nothing now but tick tick tick tick tick tick tick tick tick tick tick tick. He looked down at the tract in his hand. Read the pull quote, "So we do not lose heart. Though our outer self is wasting away, our inner self is being renewed day by day. For this light momentary affliction is preparing for us an eternal weight of glory beyond all comparison, as we look not to the things that are seen but to the things that are unseen. For the things that are seen are transient, but the things that are unseen are eternal."

Titus yelled at him, "Keep it aimed at me." His hand had fallen. He raised it again, pointed the gun at Titus' forehead. It all made sense that sense made no sense, that there was no role to play but his own. Tick tick tick tick tick tick tick tick tick. He looked down at his phone. A message from Rebecca: where are u.

What is a where? And how long could he be there? He had less than a minute to make a decision. He held his aim and turned his head away. He didn't see what happened. He didn't hear a bang. He only heard the ding, which didn't seem like it would ever stop ringing in his ears.

About the Author

MIKE HILBIG graduated in 2017 from Sam Houston State University with an MFA in Creative Writing, Editing, and Publishing. He lives in Houston, TX and teaches English at the University of Houston-Downtown and at Lone Star College.

CPSIA information can be obtained
at www.ICGtesting.com
Printed in the USA
LVHW031302191121
703773LV00001B/71

9 781948 692762